ǀNamgu's Escape Theory

Beauty Boois

UNAM PRESS
UNIVERSITY OF NAMIBIA

University of Namibia Press
www.unam.edu.na/unam-press
unampress@unam.na
Private Bag 13301
Windhoek
Namibia

First published: 2020
Cover artwork: Nambowa Malua
Cover design: Jigsaw Graphic Design & Layout
Design and layout: Vivien Barnes, Handmade Communications
Author photograph: Namafu Amutse

ISBN   978-99916-42-59-8

Distribution
In Namibia by Namibia Book Market: www.namibiabooks.com
Internationally by the African Books Collective:
www.africanbookscollective.com

To my angel Jermaine (JJ) Tjizo (26.03.1997–13.05.2019)

and

my slice of heaven on earth, Beyonce (BB) Boois

For JJ

I remember the first time I saw you
Fat cheeks glowing with a bright stare in your eyes
You were the first baby I'd seen beyond my own reflection
I was only seven but I knew that only heaven could bring us
someone so pure and true
so my affection and immediate attention is what drew me
    to you
Years went by and like a flower I watched you grow and bloom
You took all the dirt that life threw at you and grew
Despite everything you managed to pull through
Like your lotus flower tattoo you grew up toward the light and
nothing that I've ever known could shine as bright

See You had an old soul but you rarely felt whole
And I wish that I could hold you close and grow old with you
And watch you make all your art dreams come true
And I wish that I could say, no not today;
And that my words were enough
To make you call all our bluffs and jump out that box
Or that this was all a dream or a nightmare from the depths
    of hell
But alas it is not.

For when I call your phone it's not your voice beaming
    through the speakers
And when I walk past your room it's not your laugh that I hear
And when I reach out to hold your hand it's not your warmth
    that I feel
So I realize that this is really real
No more Afro curls

No more glowing cheeks
No more melodic poetry
No more you for me

But that's only in reality for your spirit soul and entire being
   I will carry
in my heart endlessly
And your smile will linger in the sun and bring me warmth
   eternally
And your caramel skin will shine through every light I see
And your creativity will live on through every sweet melody
   of your music and poetry
that radiated through your entire being
which will forever be with me
And I will carry all our memories like a sacred treasure chest
And I know that you've found peace coz your serene soul
   deserves only the very best
And Even though your heart's been put to rest,
I know that your light and your glow and your soul and your
   laughter
and your creativity and your intellect and your beauty and
   your poetry
will linger till we all turn to dust and go
beyond eternity
Because I will always carry you with me

Acknowledgements

This book is a direct result of my parents' support of all my dreams. Seth and Yvonne Boois filled my childhood home with books (some authored by my father) and unconditional love.

To my sunshine, ǀGamirob, for sharing his mother with her stories and the process it took to complete this book. I am grateful to have such an understanding and supportive soul in my life.

To my siblings who are also my best friends (Bianca, Beaulah and Beyonce) for always cheering me on and taking the time to read all my work before anyone else, even before I'd ever dreamed of having anything published!

To Jill, Naitsikile, Mutaleni and Fredrika from the UNAM press team, and three anonymous reviewers. Thank you all so much for reading and polishing this story in ways that I could not even have dreamed of. I'm so sorry for all my grammar and other errors (you've taught me that writing is about so much more than telling a story)!

To Nambowa Malua who shared his beautiful talent for the cover artwork and captured ǀNamgu just as she is.

I couldn't have written this book without some sort of grasp of the English language so I have to give thanks to my high school English teacher, Ms J., for encouraging me to write and for being one of the first people to compliment my writing!

Sometimes all you need in life is for someone to give you a shot and that's exactly what UNAM Press as an establishment has done for me! Thank you for taking a chance on a fresh voice.

One

'*Axaros*, it won't be as bad as you're making it out to be, besides, it's only for a short while then it's off to law school! Think of it this way: there shouldn't be any competition at all when it comes to graduating top of your class, maybe even top of the entire matriculating year! That will be the perk of switching from private to government school, *ama-e?*'

|Namgu's mother repeated these words every time her daughter complained about having to attend a government school where she knew nobody and wasn't interested in making any new friends, although she really felt the need for one. |Namgu already hated all her classmates, she hated the uniform, but mostly she hated her parents for ripping her away from her previous, exclusive school with its familiar routine that kept her anxiety at bay. Just as her bitter loneliness was about to manifest into tears, a short and stubby man entered the classroom. He had an extremely large belly with tree trunks for legs, and she nearly burst out laughing at the sight of him because his appearance resembled that of an Oompa Loompa working in a chocolate factory in a book she had read as a child. |Namgu managed to compose herself and disguised her chuckles as a cough.

The short, stubby man went on to introduce the topic to the tiny mass seated before him and the lesson ensued.

As the day went by, |Namgu moved silently from class to class and although her body was present, her mind was on happier days back at her old school in South Africa, where she had had a flock of friends and the time that passed between classes was filled with schoolgirl gossip and giggles. Now, during classes, if she eagerly raised her hand and engaged in intellectual debate with her teachers, her classmates rolled their eyes.

The bell signalling the end of break time rang through the school corridors and across the quad, and the learners made their way to their respective classes, some dragging their feet and taking their time, others speed-walking anxiously. It was a chilly day in Windhoek and the air seemed as though it were made of ice that could dry up your bones while the wind threatened to blow your entire life away, like a sand particle driven towards the dunes. |Namgu was the first to enter the classroom and the English teacher, Ms Janik, entered right after her.

Ms Janik beamed at her students as she took long elegant strides in her pink kitten heels to her desk. She wore a flowy pink dress that matched her shoes and her blonde hair was neatly pulled back in a pink bun. She was a beautiful woman but teaching big groups of unruly children had aged her, shown in her prematurely wrinkled face and fatigued eyes.

|Namgu returned a shy smile. English was one of her favourite subjects and she had a feeling that Ms Janik would become her favourite teacher here; something about her warm smile and energy tipped her off.

2

Ms Janik sat on her desk and crossed her legs as she watched the learners drag their feet, lazily making their way to their seats. She loved teaching but the learners almost always tested her love for them. This was one of her better-behaved class groups, which was really saying something because they were mostly very difficult and sometimes even impossible to contain. She didn't have to wait long for their noise to die down. *A good day*, she thought.

'Good day everyone, how are we doing today?' she glanced across the classroom.

'Cold!'

'Hungry.'

'Tired, Miss.'

The answers came from all around the classroom, one from a boy who slouched in his seat, another from a freckled faced girl who longingly stared out of the window and another from a boy who had folded his arms and placed his head in the nook between them.

'Well then I say, we warm our hearts, feed our souls and awaken our minds with some poetry! Last week I gave you all an assignment which you can hand to me at the end of today's lesson.'

'*Aye* miss, some of us didn't get time to do it, man.' The boy slouched in his seat exclaimed.

'*Ya etche*, a week is too short notice *jong*! Anyways, English isn't our language so how can we now *kamma* wanna come and analyse such heavy poetry?' The boy with his head on his desk looked up to ask.

'Well then, you had better listen attentively during this lesson, take some notes and make sure you get the assignment to me before the end of the school day. Otherwise, it's a fail.

I've seen the work that you are all capable of and I know it's challenging but I also know that you have the potential to write a good analysis for me, and of course, I mark all your papers keeping in mind that English isn't your mother tongue. Now, let's start our discussion. The poem you had to read and analyse is titled "Caged Bird" by the great Maya Angelou. Who can tell me about the theme and the meaning of the poem?'

ǀNamgu's slender arm shot up into the air as the girl seated behind her rolled her eyes and said, '*Wheeeew, kyk net vir* teacher's pet!' and the majority of the class tittered with laughter.

'Okay guys, let's give our new girl a chance to share, especially those who haven't done the assignment yet. Listen and learn! ǀNamgu, is it? Sorry I can't get the click right, is it okay if I just call you Namgu?' Ms Janik asked, bright-eyed.

'Sure.' ǀNamgu hated it when people asked that but she didn't want to cause any trouble so she obliged. 'Anyways, when I read the poem it made me feel a number of things, a strange mixture of sadness and happiness because "Caged Bird" seems to contrast and compare darkness and despair with light and hope. In her poem, the caged bird represents darkness and despair whereas the free bird represents light and hope. The poem seems to be about freedom and isolation, about how most people take their freedom for granted whilst there are "caged birds" or people who face life alone, crying to be seen, to be heard, to be free.' If she were being honest, the poem resonated deeply with her. She had cried herself to sleep the night that she first read it because she understood how alone the caged bird must've felt, and she understood why the caged bird sings.

'*AYE, AYE!* The caged bird isn't about those woke things, it's about getting it in. The song it sings is a mating call!' The boy using his arms as a pillow turned his head to exclaim. Half the class burst into hysterical laughter. Ms Janik's forehead wrinkled in irritation as she gestured for silence like a conductor.

'Excellent job, Namgu. I'm impressed. Someone who has independently read the poem. You may have a day in which to write the assignment. I look forward to reading your work! Everybody else, assignments on my desks, please! Those who haven't done it, make a plan and get it to me before the school day is out.' The school bell rang and the learners started packing up their belongings.

The culture of Socratic dialogue and class participation were foreign concepts in most government schools and so INamgu's enthusiasm for intellectual debate was frowned upon by her peers. In the days to come, she often heard more classmates referring to her as a 'teacher's pet', a 'know-it-all', and a 'show off' under their breaths as she walked by them. She decided that this school was the most terrible place she could possibly be.

Everything will change once the latest Xam-Khoen book is released, she frequently thought to herself, and when the day finally came, something small, yet significant did happen. Something that would one day change her life forever, not that she knew it in that moment. In the time that her world had been turned on its head by changing schools, books were the only sanctuary in which INamgu could find peace, quiet and most importantly, a companion – even if all contained within their pages was purely fictional, a figment of some far-away writer's imagination. The bounds of INamgu's imagination were ever expanding with a book in hand and beyond all that, she found comfort and resonance in them, especially in the books of the Xam-Khoen trilogy. The stories of the Xam-Khoen (Lion People) were written by a Namibian author who made it her life's work to write African Science Fiction based on mythology that had been passed on through generations of Khoekhoegowab-speaking people.

The last book in the trilogy was about a Damara hunter who became a social pariah because, unlike all the other hunters in his clan, who began shape-shifting into lions by the age of thirteen, he began transforming only at the age of 18, and instead of transforming into a male lion, he became a lioness. As is the case in many societies, what is different or strange is often misunderstood, or not understood at all, and what is misunderstood or not understood at all, is mostly rejected or denied. The underlying theme of the book was isolation and loneliness, presently all too familiar concepts to |Namgu. This made her realise more than ever, that what is in our imaginations tends to be a distortion of reality, and she took comfort in that realisation. Somehow the author of the Xam-Khoen trilogy had injected *her* reality into a fictional story. That the cause of |Namgu's loneliness and isolation in life and at school was because she hadn't made a single friend, nor taken an interest in her peers because they were different from her and she was different from them, and that neither of the two parties seemed willing or interested in breaking through those invisible barriers, had not occurred to her. So |Namgu kept her nose in her school books and during break times she indulged in an overabundance of fictional novels.

It was a windy day in the middle of July when the school bell rang and she was free to read the newly-released, latest book about the Xam-Khoen. The trilogy had become a quartet. She hurriedly ate her salad sandwich and nestled herself into a corner underneath the staircase, right next to her English class. She'd packed a little blanket into her school bag, so she was quite comfortably seated, with her back pressed against the wall, and began reading. As she did so, her imagination allowed her to travel to the dry and distant corners of the Namib Desert, to the Xam-Khoen, to the social pariah and all the other characters whom she had grown to love.

Unbeknownst to her as she read, a girl with a big mess of dark curls, round hips, and golden skin hovered over ǀNamgu, trying to get her attention for five minutes without any success until she eventually waved a chubby hand in front of her book.

'Uhm, hello! Anybody home?' she asked mockingly.

It was not an unfamiliar experience for ǀNamgu to be completely engaged when she was reading. It felt to her as though she were submerged in the depths of the pages in the imaginary realms of fiction, and it usually took a gentle touch to bring her back to reality, but the wave of the golden skinned hand between her face and her book forced her to return to her nook underneath the staircase, blinking her brown eyes up at a round face that seemed to be engulfed by the mess of curls. As startled as she was, ǀNamgu managed to open her mouth and begin apologizing. She wasn't only startled because of the way she'd been pulled back into reality but also because this was the first time since she started at her new school that anyone, beside a teacher, had spoken to her. She sized up the golden-skinned beauty: a stunning girl of average height with a head full of noticeably messy curls,

7

piercing green eyes and a uniform that appeared massively unkempt. *She must be new here too* ǀNamgu thought to herself – the rumours about her being a snob and a suck-up had spread fast. Unlike at her old school, the other students did not admire or look up to her.

'I'm so sorry, I was just…' ǀNamgu started saying when the girl who looked as though Carlos Santana had sung into life, chimed in, '… in your zone, right? I get it! I'm crazy about those books too. Anyone who doesn't believe in teleportation, has clearly never picked up an intriguing book!' She finished ǀNamgu's sentence.

'Anyway, I'm Sophia, we have history class together. I think you're exceptionally smart and not just because you get good grades, but in the way you seem to question almost everything, even the knowledge that the teachers try to shove down our throats. I know everyone gives you a hard time for it, but I know better – people always judge what they can't understand, especially the hormonal air-heads that walk these halls. Besides, I admire intellect. It's hard to come by and then you started bringing that to school and I knew that we had to be friends! So tell me your story, what's a girl like you doing in a place like this?' Sophia swung her hand around in a circular motion, an air of truth and sarcasm surrounding her, and they both laughed.

ǀNamgu couldn't believe it. She was making her first friend and someone who appeared to love reading as much as she did, an intellect! She thought that the girl standing over her was way too blasé, too forward and a little overwhelming, but she didn't care. She needed a friend, so she began to tell Sophia about herself right then and there – about the existential crises that almost every moment of her life presented, her body issues, her cultural confusion, her parents and their long list of demanding expectations topped by the never-ending comparison to her older sister, and everything in between. Overtaken by the excitement of connecting with a like-minded person, they both lost track of time, skipped all their classes and spent the rest of the school day on ǀNamgu's blanket under the staircase, learning almost every detail about one another. Their friendship grew over the days that followed, walking to classes together, sharing secrets under the staircase next to ǀNamgu's English class, talking like close cousins raised by the same grandmother, and as time grew older, ǀNamgu and Sophia forged an unbreakable bond, stronger even than the closest of family ties.

Unlike her first few weeks at school, ǀNamgu began to look forward to attending school every day, not just because of her love of learning, but also because of Sophia. As the year slowly neared its end, the icy chill of winter departed, the sun's heat grew in intensity and the leaves started to fall. One day in October, ǀNamgu stood near the drop-and-go area with a Sharon Kasanda book clutched close to her chest in one hand, and her other hand fingering her coils as she waited for Sophia, who always arrived at school later than she did.

'Hey sleepy head, you didn't even text good night last night. You okay?' Sophia said, planting a kiss on each of ǀNamgu's cheeks whilst tucking her shirt in and tying her hair up.

'Yeah, I was just super tired, dozed off watching the news,' ǀNamgu yawned as they made their way to the quad to line up for assembly.

Camelthorn High School was one of the better kept government schools because some of the alumni had set up a fund to pay for the maintenance and upkeep of the school grounds. The two girls strolled across the basketball courts from where they could see the rugby field covered in dusty brown grass. A group of students who had been smoking all the way on the other side of the field called out to and waved at Sophia.

'*Bom dia!*' she yelled and blew kisses in their direction.

'I can never get over the way you seem to know everyone at our school. Everybody loves you!' |Namgu adjusted her black backpack.

'Network determines net worth or something along the lines of nepotism meeting capitalism!' Sophia said playfully, sticking her tongue out. 'Sooo, how'd your parents take it?'

'Just like I predicted, they weren't at all happy about it. They called me a liar and a *skelm* for keeping it secret from them. I guess in a way I do understand their anger. I did submit my application behind their backs after all, so…' She shrugged as she removed her backpack and sat on one of the wooden benches along the outer edges of the quad. Assembly would only start in ten minutes, and there was enough time for them to keep talking. Sophia sat down beside her; all she ever brought along to school was a notepad, a pen and whatever novel she was reading at the time.

'So…what?'

'So, I just… get where they're coming from.'

'Well, it doesn't matter where they are coming from, *you* got into the university of *your* choice to study what *you* want to study, and do, for the rest of *your* life! It's not about where they are coming from, it's about where *you* are going. Don't feel bad about choosing yourself! I know you well enough already to know that you are feeling guilty, and second guessing your decision – you shouldn't, okay?'

'Okay...' |Namgu shrugged again.

'That's about as convincing as those kids in class who pretend to be looking in their bags for homework that they know they haven't done.' They both laughed as |Namgu leaned in to hug Sophia.

'Thank you,' she whispered as a few teachers emerged from the teachers' lounge and learners began lining up for assembly.

Two

|Namgu's mind was often plagued with philosophical reflection, especially in the mornings when she would get lost in thought staring at her own reflection in the mirror. A memory slowly pushed its way into her mind like clouds shifting above a clear blue sky...

Her mother sat in the front row of the theatre, about a stone's throw distance from the stage, aimlessly scrolling through her phone because she needed something to do so that the people around her wouldn't think that she was weird for being out alone. Hatago was not used to going out without her husband but when it dawned on her that her husband's lack of interest in |Namgu's first theatre performance would mean that she would have to come and see the play solo if |Namgu were to have any support at all, she was determined to attend it. The phone provided a way of coping with being alone.

The theatre was brightly lit and swarms of people were coming in, looking for seats or a familiar face. Some sat in silence, others took numerous selfies. The director had explicitly instructed |Namgu not to, but she desperately needed to check the theatre buzz before the play began, so she peaked through a small opening between the thick black theatre curtains.

'She's here,' she thought happily, startled when a tall man whom she recognised as one of the stagehands walked up the stairs alongside the stage with a microphone held up to his bearded face, making his way to centre stage as the theatre lights shone against his umber skin.

'Ladies and gentlemen, welcome to the Makhanda Girls' School Theatre! Please make your way to your seats, as show time is fast approaching.' He paused, and the busyness of the crowd grew still. 'Tonight we will be treated to what I can only describe as world-class acting by senior drama students from Makhanda Girls' School as they showcase "What Happens When Roses Die", originally written by Beatrice /Goagoses and now adapted and directed by Dantago Damaseb. We ask that you respect the thespians by kindly keeping your phones on silent, allowing only the actors' and actresses' voices to ring through the theatre this evening.' By the time the announcement was over, /Namgu had already taken her place on stage for the opening scene. As the stagehand turned and left the stage, the lights dimmed except for those that shone directly onto the stage. The play was about a man who had lost everything and had been sentenced to prison, leaving his wife and children to fend for themselves and face the debt that he had left in his trail. /Namgu played the role of the wife and toward the end of the play recited a poem that her mother would later inform her had given her goosebumps:

'Blood stained roses grow in places no one dares to sow.
Roses are red because their blood has been shed,
No sweet scent, for all that's left is the stench of death and
    sorrow,
No will to live for they have no promise or hope for tomorrow.
But something magical happens when the skies cry and
    roses die,

The soil becomes fuller and richer as our petals break down
    and become one
With the earth and we are given a renewed sense of life through
A new beginning, a new chance, a new birth.'

It wasn't uncommon for an actress to identify deeply with the characters played and ǀNamgu remembered feeling a strong resonance with her character at the time. They were both confused and felt abandoned, left to fend for themselves as the ones they loved turned their backs on them. Her memory triggered a stream of thoughts that were as common to her as they confused her: *Exactly what is the point of life? Of work, of play, of friends, of family, of breathing, of living, of existing? Is life just a crazy rat race that persists from generation to generation with the ever-elusive abstract concepts of peace, love and happiness dangled in our sights like carrots on a stick? Giving us just enough motivation to chase but never enough of a taste to know that the possibility actually exists for the concepts to be injected into every waking moment? Then there was the question about aesthetics: what was the purpose of beauty? Did certain types of physical features exist purely for the amusement or attention of others, or were there actual logical and reasonable, survival based reasons for the way that she looked?*

These were the thoughts that kept ǀNamgu up late at night and the reason why her mother scolded her over the breakfast table on so many occasions as the look of fatigue and maturity ate away at ǀNamgu's face, turning it into the face of an old stoic philosopher – forever contemplating life and asking impossible questions, since the day she had begun talking. So many lines etched upon the face of youth: an absolute tragedy in the eyes of Hatago Swaartbooi who all too often watched as her daughter's face twisted into a sort of morbidly pondering grimace; not the care-free face of a teenage girl. She constantly reminded her daughter about smiling more.

As she stood in her room, |Namgu stared at her reflection frowning back at her from the full-length mirror with a sense of pride, a little bit of confusion, a tinge of self-loathing and a thousand unanswered questions soaring in her head. She looked at the tight coils of afro hair that had been twisted and tangled into each other forming knots on her head, imagining how light and fluffy and cloud-like her hair would be when she untangled them after a day or so, depending on how she would feel in the coming days. She stared into the big black pupils encased by slightly slanted eyes, a round nose protruding from the face with sensuous brown lips below.

Who am I? She thought, a question that rang in her head with the sound of the voices of her mother, aunties, cousins and almost every family member that she had encountered. Her eyes moved down her naked body: a body that was never quite as thin as she had always hoped for; a hope which had been the driving force behind her regular pattern of secretive binging and purging. Her love of food had been hopelessly unmatched by her fear of weight gain and so bulimia nervosa had taken a strong hold on her for most of her teenage life, only to leave depression in its wake, a depression that was fuelled by her own skewed perception of herself, depression ignited by a world that mercilessly seemed to eat away at all hope and happiness with an insatiable hunger. Nestled within all this loomed an impending identity crisis perpetuated by typical adolescent confusion that made self-knowledge

15

seemingly impossible for the young girl staring at her own reflection.

Inside herself, the climate resembled that of Swakopmund on any given day – cold and misty in the mornings, clear, blue skies at midday, and cloudy and gloomy during the evenings. Her undiagnosed mild depression often zapped her of energy whilst her anxiety conjured enough panic and fear to keep her active in order to avoid imminent failure and quell her looming sense of hopelessness.

Her skin resembled the deepest hue of the coastal dunes like most Khoekhoegowab speakers from the south, a trait attributed to their San ancestry, much like their high cheekbones, a feature that ǀNamgu possessed too. Being from the south meant one of two things to people from the south: you were either born and raised in the south, which made you a bona fide Nama, or your parents were born and raised in the south while you grew up in the city, which made you what millennials would call a coconut. The former validated your Nama-ness and the latter made it questionable, depending on a number of factors, one of which included your ability to speak Khoekhoegowab fluently, which is where ǀNamgu fell short. Her parents, like many well-off black people who had made their way out of poverty from the smaller regions of Namibia, had for reasons known only to themselves, decided against prioritising their native language over English, and, as a result, ǀNamgu's Khoekhoegowab sounded like the gibberish a toddler learning to speak would babble. Her cousins branded her a coconut and teased her for her mispronunciation of the clicks that made Khoekhoegowab such a distinctive language. ǀNamgu thought it unfair that she'd been branded this way, which had the intention to strip her of her blackness in the name of variables over which she had no control. She couldn't choose where she'd been born, nor could she choose how much exposure she'd have to the language growing up, or how much of it she could retain. Her family made her feel alienated and isolated, like she couldn't relate to them, like she didn't belong. Which is what labels do best, they divide people. It didn't help that she was built like an ironing board or that she had picked up a posh accent from years at her swanky boarding school. INamgu struggled to learn to accept and love herself, including all things pertaining to her physical appearance, the struggle to speak her native tongue and her inability to relate to her family. She battled with these insecurities daily but managed to make up for them in her own way by over-achieving in sports, in school, volunteering, the works. Over the years she had overcome invasive inner voices and suicide ideation under the guise of a highly functional personality, and she had become brilliant at it. Since moving from boarding school permanently back home to Namibia, she found that something within her had shifted, in a small but significant way. Her friendship with Sophia had instilled in her a newfound sense of hope, and a confidence that she began to acquire through imitation.

Three

As the school year was nearing its end, many of their peers had a surprisingly calm energy about them.

'Just look at them,' Sophia waved a judgmental finger at a few students rhythmically walking toward the guidance teacher's classroom with university applications in hand. 'The brainwashing is so real,' Sophia sighed.

'Brainwashing *ti*? |Namgu laughed, '*Etoh*, how do you just decide! Maybe they've made their own choices.'

'This lot?' Sophia scoffed, '*Nooit*,' she dragged out the word in her ever-awkward Afrikaans accent and they both laughed as they sat with their backs against the wall under the staircase.

'I'm just saying, there are some of our classmates who actually seem to know what they want to do with their lives and have chosen to apply for university out of their own free will, Sophia. Not everyone wants to be a creative and it's actually a tad bit hypocritical to judge them, isn't it? I bet nobody expects you to even think of three to four more years of attending yet another institution, and yet, here you are,' |Namgu pointed to the application form attached to the clipboard in Sophia's lap, raising an eyebrow.

'Why are you always right? You're so annoying, has anyone ever told you that?' Sophia rolled her eyes as she wrote the words 'dance major' in the subject choice field of her application. 'So how'd you convince them?'

'Oppression.' INamgu shrugged as Sophia cocked her head forward, wide-eyed.

'How Sway! And what about the career assessments they wanted you to take?'

INamgu sat up straight and fixed her imaginary tie.

'Here's a word by word account of what I told them.' INamgu cleared her throat and switched over to a British accent. 'In countries all over the world, psychometric testing has been used to perpetuate lies and stereotypes about people of colour in order to keep them oppressed and stop them from progressing. Assessments were standardised for WASPS, otherwise known as White Anglo-Saxon Protestants, and Education Departments under the Nationalist Party in South Africa used adapted versions of the Stanford-Binet tests to display superiority of one race over another. It is for this reason, amongst others, that I, a black woman of colour, refuse to take any such career assessments. I thank you.'

The girls burst out laughing as Sophia applauded, yelling, 'Bravo, bravo! Dude, that's so brilliant. How did they respond?'

'You know my dad kinda shuts down whenever anyone talks about anything that goes against his will. He either backs you financially or leaves you to fend for yourself, but mom seemed to be on board. You know how she is: she'll never really have my back in front of my dad or my sister but secretly, she always seems to show up for me. After our little family meeting, she seemed to have done some research

19

and suggested that I look into majoring in both psychology and drama. She made it clear that she didn't approve but that she wanted me to have something a little more concrete and something that would stop my dad from cutting me off. I wish she wasn't always so scared of openly fighting for me but her standing up for me in secret is better than nothing.' INamgu slouched back against the wall.

'I hear you. I barely remember my mom but I suppose any version of a mother is better than a dead mother.' Sophia reached over to INamgu and gave her hand a tight squeeze, 'I'm proud of you bestie.'

After many long days under the familiar staircase together, and completing their high school education, they both enrolled in the Namibian University of Humanities and were passionate about their chosen fields. Just as her mother had suggested, INamgu chose a double major: drama and psychology.

Drama had always been of great interest to her. She loved the theatre, its energy and the endless numbers of lives that it enabled actors to live. Unlike the books that she enjoyed disappearing into, theatre offered a different type of escape, one more tangible than reading a novel. Her parents had always told her that it was a great hobby but strongly advised her to put all her efforts into becoming a lawyer. They had always presumed that she would grow out of what they referred to as a phase, but they were sorely mistaken.

Although INamgu was an extremely conservative young woman, the one area in her life where she allowed herself to be free-spirited was acting. Theatre allowed her to feel anything, to be anything, to believe anything; all she had to do was allow her body to be the vessel for the characters to pass through and she did it well. Her parents were the type of people who turned their noses up at the arts and anyone who chose the arts over something more stable and realistic. It pained them both deeply that their daughter had strayed from the path which they had always been so certain she would follow, but the more they spoke out against her choice, the more she pulled away from them. They blamed Sophia for being a bad influence on their daughter which is exactly what they told all their closest friends and relatives, every single chance they got. This, of course, wasn't the farthest thing from the truth because it was Sophia's long winded monologues and lectures about freedom and carving out one's own path that had stirred up the strength inside |Namgu to follow her heart – to be true to herself.

Sophia's life as a dance major was filled with dance workshops and auditions or late nights spent rehearsing and stretching and finessing techniques or learning new choreography. Life grew stale much too often for her liking and she seemed to be allergic to routine, so she used dance as an escape from the dull and stale aura that clung to everyday life. Unlike |Namgu's parents, her father was a very loving and supportive man, who admired his daughter for her bravery in the pursuit of her dreams. He admired her bold, outspoken nature, and the energy of a wild woman she had no doubt inherited from her mother.

Sophia grew up to become a very sensual woman who celebrated her body and freedom in every, and any, way she pleased. She fed most of her sexual desires and cared very little about society's patriarchal views about how women should behave when it came to their sexuality. She was not one to be policed or shamed. She didn't believe in monogamy and

21

sabotaged any fling that became too serious for her liking. To her, monogamy was a projection of insecurities that ruled the human psyche, the type of insecurity that sought to exert its control and ownership over others, all the while using an obscured view of love as an excuse for it all. She enjoyed the freedom of not having to answer to anybody about anything. This was one of the ways in which the two girls were polar opposites.

|Namgu was more conservative and decided to hold off having sex until she met *the one* and then, only under perfect circumstances. She was a hopeless romantic. She wanted to experience and make love to only one person. She believed in soulmates and this was the one area in her life that couldn't be shaken by Sophia's speeches – no matter how convincing she was.

When she eventually started dating in university, |Namgu and her boyfriend took a vow of celibacy together. Tangeni was perfect for her – if you believe in that sort of thing. Perfect in the sense that he never overwhelmed her. He was present enough to be noticed but too preoccupied to have any profound impact on her. He was a straight-laced, church-going young man who accepted the fact that she wasn't as dedicated to the church or his religious beliefs as he was. It was his belief that the light of the Lord would someday shine through him so brightly as to inspire |Namgu to allow his God to save her from eternal damnation; this was his heart's greatest desire. He knew this was possible because he saw in her all the attributes of a good Christian woman who had been blessed with unfaltering beauty and a heart of gold – a true Proverbs 31 Woman. Every night Tangeni dedicated his prayers to her salvation and that God would protect her

22

from Sophia whom he deemed incapable of repentance and undeserving of God's mercy, not possessing the purity of his beloved |Namgu. He mostly prayed that Sofia would not lead |Namgu into the path of what he deemed to be a life void of a moral compass, not to mention her series of sexual escapades with both men and women. He tried his very best not to judge her, but she made it so hard not to. *Judge not, lest ye be judged*; he mentally repeated the scripture like a metronome. Accordingly, he put in all his efforts to pretend to like her and to stop himself from protesting in disgust every time he witnessed yet another unfamiliar man leave her bedroom or the flat that she now shared with |Namgu.

Four

Tangeni braced himself as he climbed the flight of stairs leading up to the flat where the two young women lived. INamgu had given him a key to the flat for their anniversary, so he let himself in while holding a bunch of sunflowers he'd bought from a street vendor in Klein Windhoek.

The double story flat was spacious and an accurate reflection of both INamgu and Sophia. On the first floor was a scarcely used kitchen which opened up to a brightly lit living room in which all the walls were painted a different colour. In the living room, six black bean bags were placed in a circle, surrounding a wooden stump that served as a coffee table. A large bookshelf containing a collection of self-help, pseudo-psychology books and novels about everything under the sun filled its long racks that extended from the floor to the ceiling. Their collection included the Xam-Khoen quartet which they'd kept in mint condition and re-read whenever they felt nostalgic. In one corner was an old second-hand keyboard, and a few guitars hung on the wall – both of them played music and would often enjoy jam sessions with other art students when the mood arose. The whole flat gave the feel of an art café, with vinyls next to a record player and posters of legends like Jackson Kaujeua and Brenda Fassie.

Tangeni never liked the look of the place. He felt that it was tremendously cluttered and disorganized. It always looked a mess and he preferred order and structure. He had always assumed that the decor was done by Sophia, not knowing that it was |Namgu's idea to have all those colours painted in the flat, or perhaps he did know, but chose to stay in denial about it.

He dreamed of the day when he would propose to |Namgu and move her into his house which, as a woman, she would no doubt turn into a home with strict traditional finishes.

He placed the flowers in a glass vase and threw himself on one of the bean bags to watch a televangelist sermon on his smart phone. He knew that |Namgu wouldn't be home for another hour but he wanted to surprise her when she did get home. He had just returned from a youth camp outside Windhoek, and was heavily fatigued, but he really wanted to see her.

Just then Sophia came bouncing down the stairs in a hot pink towel, her wet hair dripping all over the floor. She was barefoot as usual and when she saw him she smiled, and welcomed him back in the most sarcastic way.

'So how many fish did you capture for Jesus this time?' To which Tangeni replied very seriously, 'Not nearly enough but there's a fish right in front of me for whom the good Lord would bless me greatly for leading back to Him.'

Sophia laughed as she walked over to the kitchen. 'Trust me, your God would take one good look at this fish and toss it right back into the ocean! I'm far too wild and would corrupt the entire heavenly system of perfection you guys are running up there.'

Tangeni knew better than to get into a religious debate with an atheist who shamelessly mocked religion. Besides that, part of him agreed with her – some people were just beyond saving. Also, according to prophecy, when the time came, only a select few would hear the trumpets summoning them to heaven and he was almost certain that Sophia would not be one of them.

Sophia took a bite of leftover pizza and proceeded to clip her toenails right at the kitchen table; her strong disregard for convention and apparently for hygiene rubbed him up in all the wrong ways.

'Shouldn't you get dressed now?' He half spat at her.

She gazed up at him for a second, knew that he was judging her and decided to play into it. 'What's the point? I'm going to have to get naked just as soon as Luke walks through the door anyway!'

Tangeni never knew quite how to respond to her when she spoke so openly about her sexual antics. Even though he knew exactly how she lived, it always threw him. He shifted uncomfortably in the bean bag.

'Uhm… ok… but, uh… wait, what happened to Steven and where'd this Luke character come from? Wow, you really move like lightning, don't you!'

The question was rhetorical and Sophia half expected it. 'Oh relax, don't get your panties in a twist! Steven is old news now. He asked me to be his girlfriend and you know that I'm not interested in anything that demands exclusivity from me. Now Luke, on the other hand, is exactly the perfect match for me right now. He's here on some German exchange programme, so he's only here for about six months, and after that I'll be rid of him. I don't know why I didn't come up with this brilliant idea of just dating these exchange guys sooner – Germany sends them out and I send them back when I'm done with them – it's perfect and applicable to any other country outside of this miniscule town where I bump into someone that I've slept with almost everywhere!'

The doorbell rang and she swung her hips in a majestic stride to get to the door. Luke was at the door with a six pack of ice cold Windhoek Lager in hand. His blue eyes lit up as he stepped in, brushed his white-blond hair back, pulled her close to him and gave her a hard kiss.

'Speak of the devil.'

You are the devil, thought Tangeni as Sophia ran her fingers through Luke's hair, past his neck, down his chest and closed them around his belt buckle.

'*Wie geht's bra?*' Luke raised his head up in Tangeni's direction but Tangeni kept his eyes fixed on his phone from which he made the best of efforts to continue watching his gospel show. He waved faintly, proceeded to place his earphones in his ears and kept his head down.

A wealthy Nigerian televangelist was conducting a sermon about purity and how virginity can be restored through confession, repentance and vigorous prayer, but that God could also restore purity through milk which the evangelist would pray over and then use to bathe the victim of sexual impurities and sins. Bathing in the holy milk would restore the female body to its natural state, the land of milk and honey, he called it, only to be entered within wedlock.

Tangeni thought about how useful this might be as content for his next prayer meeting with the youth ministry of which he was one of the leaders.

Sophia and Luke had been kissing profusely all along and when they finally came up for air, she grabbed his hand and led him upstairs to her bedroom.

Luke was a generous lover and contrary to popular belief, he was well endowed – it turned out that the myth about white men had indeed been a lie. He was an athlete, with the body to show for it, and it helped that he was intelligent too.

Sophia was a sapio-sexual and lusted after intellectual stimulation almost as much as she lusted after physical pleasure. Critical thinking and creativity, constructive dialogue through regular introspection were all qualities that she sought to develop within herself but that she also found extremely attractive. Which made sense, because unlike magnets, when it comes to human attraction and romance, like attracts like. People tend to seek companionship with other people who are a reflection of themselves. She was extremely frivolous, a hedonist, an ungovernable, pleasure-seeking, unapologetic woman, both profoundly sensual and intensely intellectual. Sophia was the type of person who lived according to her own rules as much as she could, and when she found herself in a constricting environment, she would find a way to either bend or break the rules to suit herself. The same applied to when she found herself in a situation that she deemed to be too sad or sombre. Being a social pariah, an outcast, a reject because of her ideals, never fazed her. She owned her sensuality and was quick to shut down anyone who tried to slut-shame her for the way she lived. She believed in free love and she was a die-hard feminist, just as her mother had been.

She tirelessly drank the milk of African feminist writers from Adichie to Busia and looked up to renowned activists of women's issues, the likes of Rosa Namises. She resented the invisible rules in society that were upheld by outdated and manufactured religious texts, cultures that no longer served the ever-changing groups of people that they were supposed to serve as they developed, and public officials who attacked or barred women for doing with their bodies as they wished.

The hour seemed to take forever to pass as Tangeni waited for ǀNamgu to arrive, but when she finally walked through the door, she was totally worth the wait. She was always worth the wait and she would always be worth the wait.

ǀNamgu smiled as brightly as the sun and her yellow skin had a glow to it. She was an astounding woman and in Tangeni's eyes, she was perfect. Perfect except for the small fact that she refused to accept Jesus Christ as her Lord and Saviour. It was a great tragedy, in his eyes, that someday she would spend eternity burning in the fires of hell while he would be living it up in paradise with the saints, unless he saved her.

ǀNamgu wasn't very religious, not at all actually, but at least she believed in God. To ǀNamgu, God could be found in everyone and in everything, because people and all things in existence were made in God's image and therefore everything, no matter how good or bad or religious, and regardless of whether or not we believe in God, is a reflection of God, made in God's image.

Much to Tangeni's dislike and disapproval, the only part of church services that she enjoyed was the Praise and Worship session of the apostolic church which she attended every Sunday.

She attended merely to tap into and form part of the positive energy emitted during these gatherings and most days it was that energy that carried her through the week to come. She stayed in church only for the first thirty minutes and she bumped into Tangeni, for the first time, on her way out one Sunday. She didn't care much for preaching or relying on someone else to relay God's Word to her – her whole life was an ongoing conversation with God – mostly consisting of long existential monologues on her part and unanswered questions on God's part; but she spoke to Him or Her or It; she hadn't a clue as to what God's preferred pronoun was.

Even her vow to celibacy wasn't born out of religious motivation but rather because she found the idea of sexual intercourse extremely unappealing. She wasn't sexually attracted to Tangeni and often doubted whether she would eventually sleep with him. If she were being completely honest with herself, she couldn't even envision a future with him. She cared for him deeply and appreciated his loyalty to her, maybe she even loved him a little, but above all, her overriding reason for being with him was because he was the safe and comfortable choice compared to some of the scumbags out there and he, just like the Praise and Worship sessions, filled the void, made her feel less alone, less sad and less broken.

Tangeni strode over to her from the beanbag and handed her the sunflowers he had brought.

'They're beautiful, I love them, thank you,' she said.

'Not as lovely as you though,' he smiled as he kissed her on the cheek. He told her all about his trip and all the good work of volunteering and ministering he'd done while he was away.

They caught up and eventually Tangeni thought it was time to turn in. They walked upstairs together and he waited by the door as lNamgu changed into her pyjamas. He sat by her bedside and ran his fingers through her hair until she fell asleep. Her hair was one of his favourite things about her, but only when it was thoroughly straightened, and although he never said it out loud, he couldn't wait for the natural hair trend to die down. He cringed at the sight of her kinks when they attended church together, because he thought her hair looked too wild and unkempt and he was almost certain that the members of their congregation shared his view.

He kissed her on the cheek when she fell asleep, and let himself out.

Five

Sophia woke up for her morning run like clockwork every day at 5 am and today was no different. By now her body had grown so used to running that it ached and felt extremely tense when she missed a day. She put on her trainers, black sweat pants and a neon green long-sleeved shirt. She started her favourite playlist, placed her cell phone in her armband, plugged in her earphones and set out. She loved how cold and silent the morning air was. The sting of the chilly morning wind against her face was invigorating and the sweet solitude was everything to her while she pushed her body to its limits. She honoured her morning ritual and refused to start off any week day without a good morning run. She knew the route like the back of her hand by now; it was the same route she'd been running since she and |Namgu had moved into their flat together.

By the time she got back to the flat, |Namgu was still fast asleep, as usual, and if she knew what was good for her, she'd leave her be, because, more than anything, |Namgu hated the mornings. She almost always slept in and when she woke up, she was almost always grumpy.

It was very quiet inside and the morning light shone softly through the windows creating a mystic feel inside the edgy flat.

Sophia undressed, leaving a trail of sweaty clothes behind her as she entered the shower.

The sound of the water moving through the old pipes woke ǀNamgu up as they always did, but she stayed in bed, pulling the sheets over her face. *It's way too early, how does she do it?* ǀNamgu thought to herself as rays of morning light struck her face through the openings between her blackout curtains.

Some time passed before Sophia, wrapped in her towel, flung open the bedroom door and threw herself onto ǀNamgu's bed, almost sending her phone sliding off the sheets.

'Don't think I don't know you're awake, I heard you yawning, in fact, I think the whole block heard you yawn. Get up and love me,' Sophia teased as she poked at ǀNamgu from above the sheets. ǀNamgu's bed provided an escape from the demands and confusions of existence; it represented a space of inactivity, away from the judgment of her family or the anxiety of university. Another loud yawn, followed by a groan emerged from underneath her bedsheets as she mumbled, 'I hate you. Go away!' She didn't mean it. She was annoyed but she knew that they had plans. She breathed heavily and removed the sheet from her face. Sophia only laughed.

'*Ese!* spill the tea about your new lover? Tangeni told me about your steamy kiss last night. You're going to give him a proper heart attack someday if you're not more careful.'

ǀNamgu admired Sophia for her sheer disregard of the patriarchal dictatorship that tried to police the lives of women. Sofia lived on her own terms and played by her own rules. She knew that the number of sexual escapades she had, had nothing to do with self-respect and ǀNamgu thought the way she openly explored her sexuality was a brave thing for a woman to do.

'Well, his name is Luke, he's from Germany and he'll only be in Namibia for roughly six months, which means that he is super convenient! I would say I'm in love but we both know I'd be lying,' Sophia said with a mischievous smirk on her face. 'All this talk about Luke is actually reminding me of how he depleted my energy last night. I need to eat! I'll go get dressed and you hop in the shower while we both think about where we can go for breakfast, yes?'

Although it hadn't been ǀNamgu's desire to part ways with her bed this early, she too was quite ravenous so she got up, made her bed and did as her friend had instructed. She thought they could go to the new café that had opened on Independence in the CBD. She'd heard they made amazing waffles and she was in the mood to try them out.

The café was situated above an old crafts centre that sold all sorts of handmade ornaments, from light fittings made out of ostrich eggs, to clothing made from goat skin, key rings, jewellery, anything that a German tourist's heart could desire to take home as a souvenir to show off to family back home along with a magnificent tan or a painful-looking redness, courtesy of the Namibian sun.

A da ǀhao re was filled with the smell of freshly brewed coffee and baked goods. The girls sat side by side, ensconced in the café, ǀNamgu with her feet firmly on the ground and Sophia seated on her chair like a Buddhist monk with her legs folded underneath her, floating on the chair under which she abandoned her brown *veldskoene*.

'*Is jy bang vir die goggas* and the lizards?' An old Afrikaans man in his late 50s grunted through his silver beard while gesturing at Sophia's feet.

The girls giggled and Sophia shook her head no. She always sat like that. She found it exceedingly comfortable.

It was a partly cloudy day in the city, the sun beaming brightly, every now and again hiding behind the scattered cirrus clouds that passed, and the air was light and warm.

They gazed down at streets filled with closed storefronts, taxis filling up on petrol at the service station and staggering groups of domestic workers and construction workers walking to work. The sounds of chirping flocks of birds meshed with the banging of cutlery in the café kitchen.

The city was small and everyone seemed to know everyone else, so rumours and gossip spread just as fast as the morning sun rose. In spite of this, it was a peaceful, quiet and mostly slow city.

It was a beautiful day and the girls appreciated the balcony of the café on which they sat admiring a nearly complete view of the city. Windhoek had a lazy flow about it, with a buzz and warmth that never seemed to leave the atmosphere, no matter the season.

They sat eating the waffles which lived up to the hype, ǀNamgu sipping on cappuccino and Sophia her green tea whilst exchanging stories until the morning sun grew brighter and brighter. They loved their time alone, growing in friendship. This was part of the magic of life: you go through most of your life without knowing that somebody exists, and then you meet that somebody and they become so engraved in your life that you couldn't imagine it without them.

'How are you two love birds going to celebrate your next anniversary?' Sophia asked intently.

|Namgu shrugged. 'Tangeni wants us to spend the evening in church, you know, to honour the place where we first met and to give thanks for our union and such...'

Sophia shook her head. 'Yeah, but is that what YOU want too?' It always got on her very last nerve the way that |Namgu constantly went out of her way to accommodate Tangeni and his beliefs. She wished that her friend had just a little more backbone.

'I don't know, I thought maybe we could spend the day in the botanical gardens and then have a long, indulgent dinner – you know, where we could just get a nice three course meal, drink a few glasses of wine and laugh till our tummies hurt and stumble into a cab.'

|Namgu didn't mind doing the church thing but she was fast growing tired of all the services, sermons and youth events that Tangeni manipulated her into attending. She preferred to focus on her personal relationship with God in the comfort of her own home, in her own way.

Sophia smiled at her friend, *a hopeless romantic,* she thought, and said, 'Wow, that sounds amazing, I love that idea for the two of you. Screw his plans, his plan kind of sucks, definitely stick to your guns with this one. Maybe one day I'll steal the idea, if I ever grow a heart and discover true love you know...' Sophia recoiled at the thought.

'Hey, that actually gives me an idea! Come July we'll have been friends for roughly three years – that calls for a celebration! We should do something special, right?'|Namgu's heart filled with enthusiasm. They had really come a long way since that day under the stair case.

'Now that's the content I signed up for! We should, this is probably the longest *relationship* I'll ever have – I deserve a trophy!'

'You should tweet that!' |Namgu laughed.

Six

The day that they had both been dreading finally dawned. Family gatherings were the perfect opportunity for hyper-critical family members to conduct interrogations, make judgements and ask boundless questions about things that didn't concern them. They pounced on her like Nama aunties at a funeral surrounding a large stainless-steel camping kettle thirsty for piping hot rooibos tea. They swamped her with questions about what exactly she was doing with her life, how financially feasible her chosen study and career path was, how soon she would be married and when she would start having babies. Growing up in an extended family, ǀNamgu had grown somewhat used to their invasiveness, but she still dreaded it every single time and tried to avoid family occasions as far as possible. Being engulfed by a large crowd of people only made her feel overwhelmed, anxious, uneasy and, ironically, only highlighted just how lonely she actually was. Maybe it was the sense of disappearing because of being surrounded by so many people, or the fact that she never felt any deep and meaningful connection to them.

Sophia, on the other hand, grew up only with her father and they had left their home country years ago, so when she first began attending family events with ǀNamgu, she was appalled when one of ǀNamgu's aunts asked her if she was 'sick' because she had lost so much weight since the last time she'd seen her. Sophia found their probing invasive and downright offensive, but since then, she too had grown used to attending these get-togethers, yet, like ǀNamgu, dreaded and tried to avoid them. She knew that her presence wasn't a requirement and that nobody expected her to attend these events, but she did it because she also knew how much more depressing it would be for her friend if she wasn't by her side. She knew this, not only by assumption but also because ǀNamgu made it a point to tell her and would often joke that she'd have to slit her wrists if she had to go alone. ǀNamgu had a dark sense of humour, a tool she used to mask her true feelings.

'Let's just make something up. Phone my mom and tell her I'm sick, please?' ǀNamgu pleaded with Sophia.

She knew her dad still held a grudge against her for not going to law school overseas the way her older sister Hotani had. Hotani could do no wrong in the eyes of their father, mainly because she obeyed his every wish. She never made a fuss when they moved from South Africa back to Namibia, she settled in easily, never went through a rebellious teenage phase, married a doctor from a wealthy family and had blessed their parents with two perfect grandchildren. Hotani was truly the apple of her father's eye and their mother adored her for making her a grandmother. ǀNamgu caused her parents immense amounts of worry and stress regarding her future and her current way of life. Unable to acknowledge their daughter's bravery for pursuing her passions, they thought of her as a failure, but mostly blamed

Sophia for influencing their daughter, because God forbid that their own flesh and blood would disobey their wishes.

As far as they were concerned, Sophia's privilege afforded her kind the opportunity to mess around with the future by taking gap years, and pursuing studies in the arts. Black people had a lot to prove, and much economic and social catching up to do. The fact that their youngest daughter had chosen to stray from the path that they thought would undoubtedly lead to financial success, brought them great disappointment, but mostly shame. They had convinced themselves that |Namgu would eventually put an end to her childish dreams and pursue a professional degree like medicine or law. All this, despite the fact that |Namgu was approaching her final year of drama and psychology studies, and had acted in award winning indie films and theatre plays.

Sophia fluffed up her curls, put on her golden hoop earrings as she looked at |Namgu's reflection in the mirror, and then sprawled out on the bed behind her wearing a baby pink strapless dress. There were many things that Sophia rebelled against but she knew better than to bite the hand that fed her, or to allow her friend to do just that, because she would not put her friend's parents past cutting her off financially. |Namgu's parents were almost certainly the type of people that would financially cut off their child, no matter how petty their reasoning. They had already refused to pay |Namgu's tuition fees, and if their daughter did anything to embarrass them further, they might halt any other financial support.

'No way, this one is really important. It's your sister's wedding anniversary, and we are absolutely going. We'll make the best of it because we'll face everyone together;

besides, there's free booze and food involved! Put your shoes on, we're going, even if it means I have to drag you there kicking and screaming.'

In moments like this, when |Namgu agonised over a family event, Sophia was so grateful for the only family that she'd ever truly known – her father, who was an extremely loving and open-minded man. Fernando had left his home town in Brazil after the death of his beloved wife when Sophia was only six years old.

He wanted to make a new life for his daughter and himself in what he believed was the most peaceful country in the world. He did this because his wife had been viciously killed in a gang shooting while visiting her mother in Rocinha, a *favela* in Brazil. He and his daughter grew extremely close and he supported her in every way he could. Not just in the ways that most parents believe they should support their children, but in the ways that truly counted, beyond financial support and material provision. Fernando developed an unconditional love for and acceptance of his daughter. He encouraged her dreams and opened himself up to her not only as a father but also as a friend and confidante. He had also grown to love |Namgu and admired the relationship that she had with his daughter. More than that, |Namgu was like a daughter to him. As for her parents, he thought they were far too harsh on their children, but accepted invitations to their parties to keep close to his daughter and to make sure that their condescending ways wouldn't spoil his Sophia's confidence and self-esteem. A part of him believed that the Swaartbooi family provided the type of stability that would be good for a girl who had lost her mother at such a young age. The type of stability that society claims single parents are not capable of providing; the type that society claims shapes actualising human beings.

Fernando was a simple man who enjoyed a simple life. He sought only basic comfort; luxuries were something that were never appealing to him. All he had ever wanted was to be able to own property, a small business and provide for his daughter. He did pretty well for himself, using his savings and inheritance from his wife to open a book store.

His wife had been an avid reader, a genuine bookworm and she left a trail of books in her wake when she passed away. The woman had also been a book hoarder, owning more books than clothes and purchasing new books whilst many remained unread in her collection which consisted of both Portuguese and English books from her days of teaching literature. Her books had been everywhere; under their bed, in their kitchen cupboards, in their car, even in their bathroom and of course in their toddler's room. She would often fall asleep with a book sprawled over her chest, close by her side or in her hands.

Fernando kept all his wife's books in a library for people to read but they were not to be sold under any circumstances The books on sale in his store were ordered from all over the world, depending on his customers' needs. He took great pride in his book store and it was his way of keeping his wife's memory alive. He named it *Bella's Books* after her, and it was one of Sophia's favourite places in the city. The father and daughter shared a connection like no other, perhaps because Fernando saw his wife's wondrous spirit in his daughter, or perhaps because he joyfully took on the role of both father and mother for his daughter; the reason mattered not in the face of the love, respect and acceptance between the two.

Truth be told, all the words in all the books in all the world could never be enough to describe their bond.

The girls were all dressed and ready, albeit unwilling to go. ǀNamgu resentfully held the door open for Sophia and said, 'Fine! We should leave now. The last thing we want is to be late and have everyone notice us as we arrive.'

Windhoek is a small city so it took the girls under twenty, maybe even ten minutes to get to the house where the Swaartboois lived in Ludwigsdorf. The yard was decadently decorated, undeniably magazine-worthy – what one might expect to see at a high tea. Huge white lanterns hung from the tallest trees which were strung with snow-white fairy lights to create an air of magic when turned on in the evening, with an assortment of off-white roses and lilies in crystal vases on the tables which were draped in blindingly white table cloths. The whole thing was over the top – overkill, according to ǀNamgu; elegant and sophisticated according to the majority of the guests who consisted of lawyers from the Swaartboois' law firm, as well as other prestigious figures from in and around the city who happily tucked into pastries and other finger foods. Bottles of expensive champagne decked the centrepiece of every table, much to the liking of everyone in attendance. An enormous, dazzlingly white tent shaded the entire shindig, specially designed to keep the Namibian heat at bay, with industrial fans creating a gentle breeze amongst the elegantly dressed guests. It was a spectacular occasion indeed and when ǀNamgu and Sophia noticed the delicious treats being displayed by the waiters who were dressed in all-white tuxedos, they looked at each other with mischievous smirks. They beckoned a waiter over to where they were standing and had their pick of mouth-watering finger foods. The girls both sized up the event, silently planning a strategy regarding a meet-and-greet with all the family members before they could find their table and attempt to have some fun.

The worst part about these types of events were the formalities, the fact that family had to be encountered with interest and enthusiasm. The fact that every family member expected a detailed update about your life, even though it had never been their priority to keep in touch with you. The fact that they then had the audacity to judge you or make snide remarks about your life and your choices. |Namgu and Sophia both knew that all this would ensue for at least the first half hour of the party.

Quite suddenly, |Namgu's aunt made her way over to the girls with a large, fixed smile pasted on her face in which all her teeth showed, including a golden split near her right canine. Aunt Elizabeth, or Liz, as she preferred to be called, was the younger sister to |Namgu's mother and took great pleasure in gloating over the fact that both her sons had been successfully enrolled into law school, in comparison to her sister's youngest daughter, who had chosen the life of a *struggling* artist over the guaranteed wealth and stability that the field of law would no doubt confer on her twins. *This is not America, this is Africa! Art cannot be a sustainable career choice — those things are hobbies,* she often would think or say out loud to anyone who would listen. She also gladly reminded her sister of these facts as often as she could. She was well known in the family for making the most inappropriate, inconsiderate and uncalled for comments. In the few minutes that would come, Aunt Elizabeth would live up to her reputation.

'Hello girls, how is everything? The ups and downs and unpredictability of the world of the arts! Oh I simply cannot imagine living a life filled with so much uncertainty! That's why I had to marry a wealthy lawyer! You know your uncle would be more than willing to grant you a sponsorship to pursue legal studies. There's really no shame in admitting that you made the wrong choice, INamgu my dear, you haven't fallen too far from redemption. Four or five years of law school and you'll be living in the lap of luxury like your mother and I. Imagine falling in love with a wealthy lawyer like your uncle, or a handsome lawyer like your father? I so badly want that for you.' Aunt Elizabeth was also known as a bit of a drunk who went off on one too many unsolicited tangents ever so often. She snapped her fingers at the nearest waiter who hurried over to fill her glass with more champagne. She took a swig and pressed on, without even bothering to wait for either of the girls to respond.

'You really are such a good catch, darling! All you need is a trip to the hairdressers and a little hair relaxer. Honestly, I don't know why you had to cut your hair off and grow your hair *that* way. Also, there's this new diet that's currently trending... something to do with Keto... I can't recall right now, but I think that would do you a world of good too, google it.' She was pointing long fingers with perfectly manicured, razor sharp nails in the direction of INamgu's hair and belly.

'If you ask me...' – nobody did, nobody ever did – '...it's just another money making scheme. Nowadays it's just endless ads about shea butter, aloe vera juice, coconut oil, hair regime this and that all over the show. What a load of rubbish, our hair should look clean and presentable at all times. I mean, your hair looks cute but when last did you actually wash and run a comb through it? Anyway, thank goodness, you light-skinned people can get away with almost any hair type. Turning to Sophia and poking a finger in ǀNamgu's direction, she said, 'Isn't she just the most adorable thing you've ever seen? She looks exactly like I did in my twenties, a little fatter, but the resemblance is uncanny.' Aunt Elizabeth had no problem rambling on and on for what seemed like aeons, offending every cell under the skin of whoever was on the receiving end of one of her rants. At this point, both Sophia and ǀNamgu were downright annoyed and had had about enough of the gold toothed lady that stood before them.

'Yes, she is just stunning. Good looks do run in your family, ma'am,' Sophia replied, adding the 'ma'am' as a jab to her friend's aunt who despised being referred to as such.

'Of course good looks run in the family! I've always found people who state the obvious infuriating. Anyway, I need a refill. These waiters are so slow, I think it's time I took my seat. ǀNamgu, be sure to go over to Sean and Patrick's table, they'd love to see you,' Aunt Elizabeth said, completely ignoring Sophia. She stumbled off in the direction of her husband, who waved happily at the girls, mouthing the words, 'I'm sorry.'

They watched her walk away then exchanged a look only the two of them understood and burst out in girlish giggles.

'Nicely done,' ǀNamgu exclaimed as she patted her friend on her shoulder.

'She had it coming. I'm sorry I couldn't tell her exactly what I was thinking! God, she just kept rambling on and on. What a headache of a woman. I feel sorry for the twins, shall we go over and talk to them? I reckon we've been assigned to sit at their table anyway.' Sophia planned on flirting with either Sean or Patrick, or both and maybe do a little bit more than flirt if the conversation was good enough, just to spite INamgu's atrocious aunt. INamgu knew exactly what was on her friend's mind, so she insisted that they move around and do more small catch-up sessions with the rest of the family before any flirting could take place. The girls swept through the yard, shaking hands and beaming smiles to people INamgu hardly knew or barely remembered.

Finally, Sophia caught a glimpse of her father as he walked between the last two lamp posts. Fernando Dos Santos was a man the height of a doorway, with wild spiralling curls for hair that he kept in a tight ponytail. A face full of folded lines revealed his age and the girth of his belly revealed his fondness for Windhoek Lager. He was a masculine man with broad shoulders and eyes that could make the sun cower. Sophia gazed at him and her heart filled with an immense sense of pride. She loved her father dearly and her heart seemed to stretch itself into a smile every time they were together. Even though Sophia grew up without her mother, she had never felt the loss of a parent because her father showered her with love and affection that filled the emptiness left behind by the death of her mother. Although, whilst growing up, she did at times crave to do the things she saw other girls do with their mothers. She even thought about how different her life might have been if her mother were still alive, how much happier her father might have been and how she probably may never have met the girl she called her best friend but loved as deeply as a sister. In her heart of hearts, Sophia believed that although people died, their soul, the essence of who they were, their energy, would forever linger inside and amongst the people and things that they loved and poured their energies into. Ultimately death is a natural and real part of life, just as birth is and she figured that the dead don't mourn or cry or fret, for death is only felt and truly experienced by the living, by the people left behind. Those who mourn their lost ones for longer than they should only need to awaken to the truth which lies in the fact that in the same intensity that they mourn, can be found the way to live a life filled with the energy that honours the dead through awareness and a lust for life.

Sophia ran into her father's arms and he spun her around in the same way that he'd done since she'd started walking. The father and daughter then started a conversation in their native tongue that seemed to ǀNamgu to last about five lifetimes. They spoke of university, the book store, her career, his love life, just about anything and everything under the overcast African sun. ǀNamgu stood and watched from a distance. She'd always venerated and slightly envied the relationship between Sophia and her dad. In that moment she felt no sense of jealousy though, only a deep admiration for Fernando who had bestowed the same love and tolerance upon her that he showed towards his daughter. Fernando felt ǀNamgu watching them, held his arms out and she ran towards him imitating Sophia and the three hugged and giggled like toddlers. The other guests at the party slithered about, whispering and pointing fingers at them though secretly dying to be cheery and light-hearted. Being of a high social standing had its perks but was suffocating and restrictive and there was barely any social space that allowed for such outlandish displays of affection. The three cheerfully helped themselves from the nearest elaborately decorated table which held a variety of delectable finger foods. After a while, they made their way over to the head table where ǀNamgu's parents were seated.

Hatago Swaartbooi wore an all-white halter dress that hung loosely below her feet and hugged her slender figure in all the right places with diamonds sparkling against her wrist, neck and dangling from her ears. She was an absolutely stunning woman with cheekbones sculpted by the gods themselves. Mr Swaartbooi sat beside his wife wearing an all-white linen suit with a tumbler of whisky in one hand whilst his other hand rested on his pot belly.

'Mom. Dad. It's uh, very nice to see you. You both look so lovely,' ǀNamgu said through a weak smile and a pained face. Ever since she defied her parents' wish for her to study law, their relationship had become quite estranged. ǀNamgu leaned in and gave her mother a cross between an awkward hug and a kiss. Mr Swaartbooi shook hands with them and welcomed them to the party. He then pointed a stubby finger in the direction where Hotani sat beside her husband and encouraged them to go over and congratulate them. As they walked away Mrs Swaartbooi shot a look over at her husband and spoke through her teeth to him,

'Was that really necessary? When was the last time you've seen your daughter?' The question was rhetorical. She was well aware of the fact that her husband had all but completely distanced himself from their daughter. She continued, 'They were barely here for five minutes and you just sent them away. You know, she might not be whatever it is we want or expect her to be, but she's still our daughter and she still needs our love and support.' Mrs Swaartbooi always had a

49

soft spot for her youngest daughter, even though |Namgu almost never did anything she and her husband asked of or expected from her.

'The girl is okay, she will be fine,' blustered Mr Swaartbooi. 'Actions have consequences. It's a tough lesson but she must learn.'

The thing that people, including and maybe especially her husband, failed to understand, Hatago Swaartbooi thought, was that love allows you to cross a thousand oceans in spite of itself because love will forever await your return, love will always pray for you, wish you well and love will always be at home, right where you left it. Mrs Swaartbooi admired her daughter's attempted free spiritedness. She quite envied her passion and determination to go out on her own and pursue a dream that all the important people in her life thought so little of. The guilt she had had about treating her daughter like a second class citizen ate her up inside but for the most part, or at least to the outside world, she had to stand by her husband; that was the African way! |Namgu was fragile, sensitive and easily saddened, something that Mrs Swaartbooi had pretended not to notice and silently wished away, because depression just wasn't a 'black' thing. She secretly wished that her husband would put his pride aside and seek out his daughter's forgiveness. She knew that it would be a hard thing for her husband to do because the man clung onto his pride as though it were an oxygen mask that pops out in the aeroplane during an emergency. He simply rejected anything that went against his perspectives. Mr Swaartbooi refused to soften his heart toward his daughter's acting talent, let alone acknowledge it. The thing is, as mothers often do, Mrs Swaartbooi loved her husband more than she loved her children. Besides all that, the reality of the matter was that she knew he would never change and thus he would never make things right with their daughter. She would have to back him, no matter what.

Being a woman of circumstance, she wished for her daughter to end up living a similar lifestyle, but she knew that pursuing a career in anything else would be the slow death of her daughter's beautiful spirit. She secretly attended all of |Namgu's shows and even drove her to some of her auditions. Seeing her on stage, being in the presence of her daughter's talent, gave Mrs Swaartbooi absolute clarity that her daughter was destined to be an actress. Although she wouldn't dare admit that in the presence of her husband, she knew it to be true in her heart, mind and soul.

Mrs Swaartbooi smiled to herself as she looked around trying to spot a glance of |Namgu when she saw her and Hotani engaged in what looked like the most uncomfortable interaction on the planet. In that moment Mrs Swaartbooi shifted her gaze toward the ground beneath her. She knew that she and her husband were to blame for all the animosity between their daughters. They had always made the girls compete for just about everything from attention to affection and praise which had resulted in the cold relationship between the girls, who behaved more like distant acquaintances than biological sisters. Hotani was their first born child, the apple of their eye, the one who received their undivided attention, their love-child. Between their birth order and Hotani's obedience, |Namgu never stood a chance. She would always lose in comparison to her older sister, and the fact that her parents never tried to hide their favouritism put a strain on the entire family dynamic.

Hotani always found it particularly difficult to connect with, let alone understand her younger sister. She was so different from her and most of the time she thought that |Namgu was the way she was and did the things she did, for attention. Who could blame her – from the moment she was born the two of them were in competition, pitted against each other for the ultimate prize of parental devotion and warmth.

'Well, thanks for coming and do enjoy the party,' she said as she gave |Namgu an awkward pat on the shoulder. What Hotani failed to grasp was that, in her bid to gain her parents' approval in almost every sphere of her life through unfaltering obedience to them, she had lost pieces of herself, her freedom and alienated her sister in the process.

'Sure thing, how are the kids?'

'Desperate for cousins and an aunt who is actually present in their lives.'

'Did you ever think that maybe, just maybe, I'd come around more if you weren't always so judgemental or if you took at least one day off from being so condescending?' |Namgu's effort to play nice was failing dismally.

'I'm your *ousie* |Namgu, I actually care about you. I have to look out for you, make sure you're making the right choices and put you in your place if need be. Mom and Dad deserve better and you know it.'

'Wow… so you're blatantly saying that I'm not good enough for the people that brought me to life?'

'*Ese* |Namgu, must you always be so sensitive? That's not what I meant, you're just overreacting. Mom and Dad love you, so do I, we just wish you were a little more like us, you know, so we can be closer. Anyways, I'm sure this phase will blow over and you'll start behaving more like a Swaartbooi someday soon. For now, let's try to have a good time and make sure your friend stays in line tonight, okay?' Hotani always knew just how to get under |Namgu's skin and always cut off an interaction in a way that allowed her to have the last word, so she walked off leaving |Namgu rubbed up the wrong way. |Namgu shook it off and went to find Fernando and Sophia on the dance floor, dancing to a genre of Angolan music that had grown in popularity in the city and in the hearts of many Namibians. Eventually Fernando had had enough of the festivities and kissed the girls good night. As the night grew older, champagne continued flowing, and spilling, and the guests slowly began to loosen up, talk a little louder and dance a little closer. The girls danced till their feet ached and their bellies tingled from laughing at watching older family members dance.

By the end of the night, Aunt Elizabeth's precious boys found themselves eating out of Sophia's hands and following her every move, as though the secrets of the universe were neatly nestled between her thighs just beyond the place where they rubbed against each other. Although Sophia never had any intention of leaving the party with either of them, she enjoyed the looks of distaste Aunt Elizabeth threw her way. When the party ended, the girls left with their shoes in their hands and laughter lingering on their lips. In spite of their hesitancy to attend the party, they had surprisingly had a pretty amazing time and fell asleep talking about the goings-on of the night.

Seven

The air was thick and tense on campus, as exams were nearing, so student stress and anxiety was rife. Most students left studying until the very last minute, some even just until the night before an exam. Sophia was one of them, INamgu, not at all; she prepared for exams throughout the year with the focused concentration of a Zen Buddhist. Sophia had a mind that worked extremely well under pressure. She fed off the adrenaline, the excitement and possibility of earning a distinction with just one night's worth of studying. INamgu on the other hand was extremely neurotic when it came to her studies. Anxiety and the fear of failure drove her to study beyond what was needed but it made her feel calmer, more in control.

The girls were on their way to attend the last lecture of the semester and when they got to class, INamgu sat in the front row, took out a notebook and pen and began writing the date on it in the right hand corner, followed by a summary of what they had discussed in the previous lecture.

Sophia sat at the back. She didn't like to sit within eyesight of the lecturer in case she got bored and wanted to slip out or in the case that she needed to take a nap or scroll through her favourite social media app. She thought that apps like Facebook and Instagram were for braindead zombies who had nothing to do but flood each other with fake-deep, pseudo-wisdom, quotes that they would never live by, and trolls. She also refused to join apps or sites that encouraged narcissistic, braggart tendencies. Twitter was for the intellects, for people who could carry decent rhetoric and where people weren't afraid to be authentic or piss each other off through well thought out dialogue. She was already scrolling away as the lecturer walked in.

The Psychology of Art lecturer was a tall, slender man in his late 50s with greying hair and kind sparkling blue eyes. Dr Leppen's presence was light and warm and his love for teaching showed by the way he interacted with his students, how he presented his lectures, as well as his enthusiasm and passion for art and psychology. Having a hand at shaping young minds, moulding them and injecting in them love and passion for art was something that he believed to be his calling in life. He found profound purpose and meaning in it and was positively charged by the creativity, excitement and nuances of youth. He thought that it kept his mind sharp and his spirit youthful. On this particular day he wanted to speak on the purpose of art in life. Being fervently theatrical, he came to class dressed as a jester from the Medieval ages and as he walked in he heard the students giggle, whisper and watched their faces light up as some took their phones out and asked him to pose for a selfie with them as he passed by their desks, which he did without hesitation. When the commotion grew old and the students settled down, he stood in front of his students and asked the question, 'Does art imitate life or does life imitate art? Are we in agreement with some studies linking creativity to mental illnesses and the ever notorious opinions of researchers, claiming that art and creative expression are an outlet for neuroses? Do we use art as one of the defence mechanisms like regression, denial and displacement? Is art indeed a method of projecting neurotic energy into something that most find socially acceptable? And who are we to say that the bearers of those observations are incorrect in their stance? Aren't the most outrageous, outlandish and eccentric people artists? Take Lady Gaga, for example. Does showing up to an awards show draped in raw meat seem like something that someone of sound mind would do? Alas her stage name in itself implies madness. Or are we to assume that the entire thing was an expression of art?'

'*Aye* sir, that chick is just being herself, man! She wore that meat coz she's a piece of meat, just like all those Hollywood prostitutes. All they do is tempt men and act crazy, that's *mos* not art. But *ja*, like they say, meat is meat and man must eat!' A pale faced young man with dirty blond hair, sitting slouched in his chair, interjected in a clear deep voice.

Dr Leppen scratched the nape of his neck.

'Interesting perspective, Thomas. Anyone have anything they'd like to add to that?'

I'm too tired for this shit. Sophia rolled her eyes.

'*Your silence will not protect you.*' She could almost hear Audre Lorde's serene yet stern voice whispering to her, and it gave her a chill.

Still tired though, and he's not worth it. Some people are just problematic on purpose; I should tweet that. Sophia lowered her head and proceeded to type her current thought process onto her Twitter feed.

'I think Thomas is right! Artists in Hollywood should conduct themselves in a respectable manner,' Nangula blurted out arrogantly.

Dr Leppen nodded. 'Well, one might argue that respectability is relative or that it takes the back seat when it comes to expressing the authentic self, no? Take Jung and his followers. They were avid worshippers of art: they asserted that art in its various forms of poetry, drawings, theatre, music and such, were an expression of the personal and collective unconscious, as a form of cultural expression. What's more, we have the work of Myers which links certain personality types to creative expression. As far as I'm concerned, the only relevance that art has, lies within its potentiality for healing, so whether all those theories and assumptions are correct or not, doesn't faze me. The job of the art psychologist, drama therapist or music therapist is not in reciting theories and making arguments based on the wisdom of old men and women who no longer occupy this world – that is the work of the academic and, of course, knowledge to be consumed by the lot of you. I, however, am in the business of painting wider horizons, writing heartfelt poems and singing more soulful songs in the minds of the young and as such, am in the business of occupying myself with the purpose of art in healing. In this case, is my opening question relevant? Does it matter which imitates which? Art or life? Life or art?' Dr Leppen paused and allowed his gaze to pass over the students, some of whom had one hand scrolling through their phones underneath their desks. Others looked as though they were stuck in another dimension. Some were taking naps and a select few had an attentive spark of awakening in their eyes.

Nangula had her hand raised up high and seemed to be struggling to keep a fountain of verbal diarrhoea from escaping from her mouth, so she pursed her lips tightly, as she eagerly shook her arm and waved her hand just a little so that the lecturer would notice her.

Oh Lord, here we go. Dr Leppen felt annoyed by his most studious yet equally annoying student. She produced only distinctions but she spoke over other students and behaved as though she was better than everyone around her. The girl had a pompous air about her and the lecturer had a particular disdain for this type of student. He reluctantly nodded his head in her direction. She responded condescendingly.

'With all due respect sir, I must disagree with you! It does matter. Without those theories, our subject matter wouldn't exist and also, I would say, that it is particularly obvious that it is art which imitates life and not the other way around. Art is a derivative of life. Life must first exist in whichever form, human beings, animals, nature and so forth, and thereafter human beings use life in all its forms to create art. If all life ceased to exist on earth, then where would the art emerge from? Who would create it? Who would even speak of it?'

The professor stroked his beard and tilted his head slightly to the side. 'Indeed Nangula, one simply cannot draw a bowl of fruit if there is no fruit to begin with.'

'*Iyaaaa, kyk vir* low hanging fruit,' Thomas laughed loudly, pointing at Nangula as a few other students joined him in laughter.

'Relax guys, Nangula brought a very concise and clear perspective to the table, although she neglected my final thought, about the role of art in healing emotional and

58

mental scars or trauma… I'm guessing you've deliberately avoided the mention of healing – which is why most students manage only to obtain the passing mark when it comes to examinations and other assessments. You students tend to be obsessed with theoretical knowledge and cling to it as though it were a life jacket which will save you from drowning or being engulfed by the crashing waves of the ocean of wisdom. I ask you this, what good does it do you, for you to know and to study the weight and anatomical composition of a life jacket, yet know nothing about the practicality of wearing it in the first place? Yes, our subject matter comprises theoretical knowledge but if every time one of you sits with a patient or client in your practice, all the theories in the world won't do either of you an ounce of good *if* you neglect what the client is actually seeking and that is, healing. So, students, with this in mind, what can be said about the practical uses of art in the healing process?'

The lecturer paced up and down the front row, eyeing the students as he did so. Nangula appeared to be flushed and he caught a glimpse of Thomas looking down the cleavage of the busty student in a red shirt seated next to him. His eyes paused upon INamgu's face. Dr Leppen thought that she was one of his brightest students. She had remarkable insight and often responded in a way that was inclusive of both academically sound knowledge as well as practical action. She was another straight A student, but unlike Nangula, she spoke only when necessary. She thought her contributions through and worked from a perspective that included logic, reason and empathy which stood at the mountain top of all healthy psychotherapeutic relationships. She would make a fine psychologist but despite all his encouragement, she had chosen the path of art exclusively and seemingly could not be swayed. INamgu returned his gaze. 'Dr Leppen, if I may?' He nodded solemnly and she continued. 'First the therapist must consider the needs of her client, before imposing any type of therapy or theoretical understanding onto that client. She must examine, observe, and be empirical as well as intuitive. She must float between the grounding of her theoretical knowledge and above towards the heights of empathy, insight, unconditional acceptance and positive regard for her client. The art psychologist should not jump to conclusions, but like the theorists and practitioners of old that came before her, she must thoroughly examine the mind, emotions, and aspirations of the human being on the couch before her. For example, if I had a client in front of me who had broken down in tears because they struggle with abandonment issues as a result of childhood neglect, some theory would advise me to maintain a blank slate, to simply listen and not react, but I might sense that someone like that might be in dire need of emotional warmth, affection and human touch, which would move me to go over and give them a hug, because I would allow my own human experience to inform my treatment of that client.'

'Oh my gosh, that makes so much sense, coz if you don't allow yourself to feel something in a session, it's like you're a robot and the client might think that you don't even care about them or something,' the busty student in the red shirt exclaimed.

'Yeah, exactly! Anyways, as I was saying, like an artist, she must open and expand her mind and be like the flexible paintbrush that needs only a gentle dip in cleansing water and can then again be used to paint various colours across the blank canvas that lies before it, ready to be guided and directed to express, to create, to direct the motion and flow of its own life. In short, art is life and life is art – the matter of imitation is a fallacy and a distraction to the therapist who wishes to empower and heal through art. Look at artists like Maya Angelou and Pink who have used poetry and songs as an outlet or a means to express their emotional distress and trauma.' ǀNamgu spoke with a deeply committed air, the words flowing from her like a stream making its way toward the ocean. She had a way about her that radiated the type of wisdom that old souls, sages and traditional healers possessed. She had a gift, a spark, a flame that burned bright and the other students felt it.

The moment she began to speak, the sleepy awakened, the eyes that were glued to their cell phones were now turned in ǀNamgu's direction and the ones who had travelled to other dimensions had found their way back to the lecture hall, beaming up at her or with open admiration. Even Thomas shifted his gaze to ǀNamgu.

'Profound, Ms Swaartbooi, your wisdom precedes your age by far. Students like ǀNamgu over here aren't concerned with being right, or the best, or first in line, but in the best interest of their hypothetical clients – and that is what makes a good therapist. That is the essence of therapy – that the psychologist offers non-judgmental, unconditional positive regard and acceptance. Complete acceptance of the flaws, the fears, the tears, the ugly calloused feet, the lies, the cheating, and the self-inflicted pain, the repetitive cycles of self-destructive behaviour – everything. See my dear students, the art lies not in name-dropping of theoretical knowledge and relying solely on that to bring forth progressive change toward self-actualisation or a state of being free from neuroses, but rather to be client-centred, to allow your client to be completely human and also for you as the psychologist to show that you too are human, just like them and not some theory dropping, holier-than-thou machine that knows everything and can do no wrong. Alas, in the end what enables the therapeutic relationship is human connection. It is with these thoughts that I wish to end our time together this semester and to remind you all that...' He looked intently at ǀNamgu, '...you have the next five months to specialise solely in art therapy which will put you on the path to becoming registered art psychologists with the Psychology Board of Namibia. I wish you all good rest and relaxation as you prepare for your upcoming examinations.'

Dr Leppen took a bow and the room echoed with vibrant applause and laughter which began to die down as Dr Leppen left the lecture room, gesturing for ǀNamgu to follow him.

'So, did you apply? Have you even considered it?' Dr Leppen walked so fast that ǀNamgu practically had to speed-walk to keep up with him.

'Sir, it's not that simple. Also, I looked at the requirements and I don't think I would get it; I mean, what are the chances?' ǀNamgu panted, trying to catch her breath.

'I think you stand a good chance, at either getting into psychology solely or taking a leap of faith and going for the big guns! You will never know unless you try. Look, just have another look at both applications. I've emailed you everything you need.' Dr Leppen slowed his pace and stopped to look at her.

'I will, I promise,' |Namgu already felt a pang of sadness over what she thought would be a rejection letter in response, but returned a weak smile to her lecturer.

'Good, and you know I'll know if you don't apply, right? Best of luck with the rest of the semester, and goodbye for now.' He chuckled and walked in the opposite direction as |Namgu waved at him.

'Thank you, Sir,' she said out loud, 'for confusing me,' she whispered, trying to catch her breath when Thomas pushed up against her from behind.

'*Ai*, sorry man. Didn't see you there, but I'm happy to bump into you! You said no last time I asked but you were *mos* busy with rehearsal *shandies* that time, so I'm giving you another chance. A *bra* hooked me up with his account so we can have a *lekker* Netflix and Chill session there by my hostel room, maybe tonight, *wat se jy?*'

|Namgu took a few steps away from him, crossing her arms.

'*Ai titse*,' she thought, rubbing her brow, a little annoyed. *When is he going to stop ohg?* 'Sorry Thomas, I don't think so. Uhm… exams are coming up, so we both have tons of studying to do. Also, you know I have a boyfriend, right?'

'So what? I just wanna chill with you. It can even be our special secret *mos,* just think about it. Get my number from the class group chat, then you let me know.'

'Thomas, I really don't thi…'

'Shh!' Thomas placed a bony finger over his lips. 'Just… text me.' He pulled her into a one-sided hug and walked away before she could finish her sentence.

63

Eight

After shucking off Thomas's unwanted advances, ǀNamgu joined Sophia, and the two friends sat side by side in the small campus theatre café. They ordered green tea for Sophia and coffee for ǀNamgu. Unlike most students, Sophia hated the taste and smell of coffee and couldn't understand the unconscious addiction that people had toward it. For her, herbal tea was like peace and wellness in a cup, a healthy indulgence and she was glad to be forever void of the smell of musty coffee breath. Above all, the leaf infused tea made her feel lighter and more relaxed, so she clung to it and wished ǀNamgu would drink it too. They sat in a rather dimly lit corner in the theatre café, the walls of which were covered in posters promoting plays, theatre movement pieces and dance shows, as well as magazine and newspaper clippings of the works produced by students of the university. The space had a comfortable, quaint feel about it, the air was warm and, unlike the rest of campus during exam times, the students seemed to be more relaxed around these parts.

It could be assumed that the thespians and students of the theatre and arts departments were the only ones in the entire university who were on a path that they had not only chosen for themselves but had also fought their parents tooth and nail to convince them to let them enter the fields of the arts. To convince African parents that artistic dreams and pursuits were worthy of their time and money was an art in and of itself. The idea that most African parents had was that the arts were for social rejects, hippies, drug addicts, low-lifes, and unintelligent people who had very little, if any, ambition and who didn't have a promising future that could boast financial success or any form of stability. Perhaps that is why the air in and around the art and theatre department was more relaxed, lighter, happier – because its inhabitants were passionate and absolutely in love with their chosen fields, willing to sacrifice parental approval for their artistic dreams.

Sophia hated the fact that parents imposed their societal judgments as burdens upon their children's minds, crushing their hopes and aspirations with their pessimistic, self-decided realism. The irony was that art used to be such an integral part of African culture. Celebratory and ritual dances, sculpting and other artwork were commonplace, as were stories told in the form of song in order to pass along important information from one generation to the next through the oral tradition. Alas, as the people were torn away from their land, language, and tradition, most seemed to have lost their desire to create, thus burying their artistic nature. After the struggle for independence, a new struggle had emerged in its place; the struggle for financial freedom and economic liberation. Which is what sat at the core of the narrative that African parents tried to force-feed their children; it was about survival. Sophia often spoke fondly about rebellion to whomever would listen and saw herself as some sort of advocate to those struggling with feelings of guilt for having defied their parents' wishes by either dropping out of medical school, or law school, to follow artistic pursuits or by being completely dishonest about their truth. Sophia's father had instilled in her from an early age the belief that each person had their own unique path and journey, a calling, something that was bigger than money, bigger than themselves and that it was one's highest duty in life to pursue one's dream relentlessly by living one's purpose in line with the meaning of one's life, the reason for existence. People spend so much time in their work places, forty hours a week, thousands of hours a year – she had to choose wisely, not that she, or anybody else couldn't change their mind at any given time, but it was best to choose what's right the first time around if possible. She felt her vocation should be a place where she could reach her fullest potential, and grow, both professionally and personally.

On the other hand, she also knew that in some instances, children tended to choose a path that was not their own in the name of rebellion or spite. To prove a point to their parents, just for the sake of defying them – that too was something that Sophia frowned upon, which is saying something, because there was very little that Sophia looked down on, or so she thought. She made it a point to always keep herself in check, a sort of self-audit on her defiant nature, her rebellion against the opinions of others, their unsolicited judgements, the conventions and taboos that existed in society. She had to construct her life in such a way that her meaning and purpose manifested itself fully, without the alteration and hindrances of either trying to submit to and obey the status quo, or going against the grain simply to display her utter disregard for living within the norms and standards set by invisible hands.

'INamgu, are you being honest with yourself? I mean, I know you don't like to talk about it but don't you think that it's getting out of hand now? You've proved your point. You didn't follow the path set out for you by your parents! If you chose to do what we both know you're destined to do, the thing that gives you life, the thing that allows you to help people in the best way you know how to; you would combine your love for psychology and drama.' Sophia spoke in a stern and serious tone, not one that she would often use.

Even though INamgu was annoyed that Sofia had broached the subject, she knew that it was time to give the matter some serious thought, or at least agree to a conversation about it. If she had the conversation, it would mean that she would have to give the issue some meaningful thought, and if she gave the issue some serious thought, then that would force her to be honest with herself and those around her. Acting was her passion. Her heart truly sprang to life with every characterisation, impersonation and script or audition. Initially, she had only gone into acting because she didn't want to study law, and at the time she wanted to do the thing that would upset her parents the most. She had ended up falling in love with the theatre and any lecturer of hers with enough time at hand, would rave about just how increasingly talented she was becoming as an actress. For the longest time, especially during her first year at the university, she had revelled in the rebellious defiance of her parents' wishes and felt in some way sure that she had made the right choice in avoiding entering a profession which was ultimately what they had wanted, until she attended her first 'Introduction to Psychology' lecture. She'd heard some of her family members say things like *the only difference between a KFC box meal and a Humanities degree is that the KFC box meal could feed a family of five.* Sophia thought that it was hilarious. |Namgu thought it hurtful and insulting.

The question of whether she was an artist, or an academic, had weighed on her mind for years. In the world of humanities where art and intellectualism often coincided, she felt confused, her heart being pulled in two different directions, her soul yearning for both, her socialisation telling her that she could have only one, her heart wanting to have it all, to do it all, to be it all. In a way, her prayers had been partially answered at the university, as all art students were required to have at least two psychology modules, because the foundations of their artistic work were based on the earlier works and methods of Stanislavski thus requiring a thorough knowledge of human emotion, thoughts, behaviour and expressions. Stanislavski's method was a technique of training actors to embody the emotions of characters to make them more believable. Following his method required a thorough knowledge of the human emotions, behaviours and psychological processes which intertwined the worlds of acting and psychology for |Namgu in a way that seemed almost perfect.

Ultimately though, she would have to choose between the two. She couldn't stay stuck between both the scientific and artistic enterprise, mingling in the irony that in many scientific circles, psychology wasn't taken very seriously as a science at all. Its origins were mostly to blame, having been derived from philosophy, physiology and lastly, the very thing that would doom the field to be seen as 'lesser than', religion.

The early definitions of psychology were from the study of the soul, the word in itself originating from Greek philosophy, 'psyche' meaning butterfly, or something of the sort, to the great debate between its being the study of the mind, or unconscious thoughts, versus observable behaviour and, and, and. What type of scientists were these psychologists if they could not even define what they were or what they studied? All of these processes just made her adore psychology even more: it was ever changing, too dynamic to grasp or define with absolute certainty, or to understand, even with all the theories in the world.

'Remember how I raved about psychology after my first lecture in first year? I was absolutely and very unexpectedly smitten. I loved it!'

'How could I forget? You wouldn't stop talking about it for days on end. I couldn't get you to shut up about it,' Sophia rolled her eyes and they both laughed. lNamgu thought back to her first encounter with psychology. The heat of the beginning of the year lingered in the atmosphere and the refreshing excitement brought about by the first years rang in the air as cheerful as Christmas bells. The lecture took place in a hall that was named after Captain Hendrik Witbooi in honour of his stand against colonialism.

The seating arrangements were like seats in an amphitheatre, levelling up the further back you went, like a set of huge steps in a half circle facing a large screen for projections, a brown podium with a thin microphone as well as a desk and table for the lecturer. The lecturer was a short, chubby woman who was dressed in an African print dress, her hair covered in an oversized *doek*.

The lecture was based on the origins of psychology and the various schools of thought within the field ranging from Roger's humanism to Watson's behaviourism, Beck and Ellis's cognitivism and Freud's psychoanalytic stance. ǀNamgu had always been curious about the complex nature of human beings and so she became smitten with humanism, which emphasized the study of the self and was a sort of rebellion against some of the other schools of psychological approaches. Deeper than that, she became enthralled by the various ways in which a human being could be dissected in terms of their actions, thoughts, feelings, upbringing and environment. What amazed her most about the study of psychology was the resilience of the human spirit, the potential for malice and the possibility of self-actualisation possessed by all mankind. She loved how science and emotions could dine together to produce this unique field of study that she so desperately wanted to embrace.

'I love acting, everybody knows this, and I was born to do it. I have a gift! I can't just give that up. You've seen how I light up when I'm on stage. This isn't about my family, Sophia, and you're right, I wouldn't be following the path that they'd set out for me. In their eyes, I would still be inadequate… You know how it is, how people see psychologists as inferior to psychiatrists here in Namibia – what's the thing they love to say? *The psychologist is the poor man's psychiatrist! The psychologist is not a medical doctor and as such, cannot prescribe medication nor does she earn as much money as the psychiatrist.* That's how they would shit all over the idea of me pursuing a degree in psychology, after celebrating how close it comes to their dream for me – *at least she's left her artsy fartsy nonsense behind* – they would say.' |Namgu circled her coffee with the spoon she was holding, with her eyes downcast. She was no longer annoyed that Sophia had brought up the subject, now she was just confused.

'And what would *YOU* say? Or don't you have a say in your own life? Are they the only ones whose opinion matters in all this or may I also chime in?' It was Sophia who was now annoyed and her irritation could be heard in the tone of her voice. She took a quick sip of her tea and continued, 'You're right, you do have a gift for acting but in all honesty, we both know you don't need to have a degree to act in a play or a film. You've got the talent, you've got some formal training from your years here and that's more than you need. Can we consider for a second that some people, people like you, have many talents, more than one calling in life and that unlike the world would have you believe, you *can* have it all and you can *do* it all.' Reading her friend's thoughts she continued, '|Namgu, your dreams are valid. You owe it to yourself to chase them relentlessly and rain down hell fire on anybody that stands in your way. You love the arts and you love psychology, so combine the two, become a drama therapist or a clinical psychologist that stars in movies and plays. Legally speaking, nobody can stop you. Spiritually speaking, the only thing that stands in your way is you and the bullshit story you feed yourself about why you can't have it all. You should apply. Dr Leppen made it clear that there's still time. Bottom line is that you can't let your parents control you and make choices the consequences of which will be yours solely. These small moments make up part of your whole life. Your duty is to fill these moments with the things that ignite your mind and set your soul on fire. Happiness is earned |Namgu, and sacrifices must be made, whether it's the respect of your family or your pride. It won't be easy, but it will be worth it in the end.' She knew that her friend had a burning passion for psychology and besides that, she knew that she would make a great psychologist.

The two friends sat in silence, taking in gulps of their warm drinks and nibbling their cake as they watched a range of students in costume enter the theatre carrying instruments in and out of the music room, and witnessed a random short bout of choreography. Just as they were leaving, they ran into a fellow drama student that Sophia had told |Namgu about. Khoënhoandias was a slim and leggy Nama girl, with a round face and big hazel brown eyes. She had her hair tied up in a tight high bun and when she smiled, she revealed a mouth full of perfectly white teeth as she waved, fiercely walking in their direction.

'*Madisa* |Namgu, *tae-na tae*? *Ola* Sophia, haven't seen you two much lately. Exam stress scare you guys off? It's crazy, right? First the lecturers are no-shows and cancel classes at the last minute, then they dump a shit-load of tests and assignments and pop-quizzes and random improve sessions, the works, and the next thing you know, it's exams, and here we are. I swear to God my head is about to explode. Anyway, that's why Veripi and his friends are throwing this huge party tomorrow night. Will you two be there? I'd really love to see you both there, especially you, Sophia, no offense |Namgu but you know I've got a bit of a thing for her.'

Khoënhoandias winked at them. Everyone knew about the on-again, off-again fling that she had had with Sophia. She was known for her fast paced speaking and it seemed like she didn't even stop to breathe as she talked. For some reason this was much to Sophia's delight – the woman that stood before her had a complete disregard for the rules of the English language or anything that she'd been taught in her voice and speech lessons at the university.

'We're good, and yes, you're absolutely right, about everything – it's a shitty little rat race they've got us running in, but I love the thrill of it. Send me the location and we'll be there.'

INamgu was already shaking her head with objection written all over her face. She had never been a fan of the social scene. Being out at bars, clubs and parties made her feel grossly uncomfortable. She often found herself feeling overly self-conscious, and wanting to go home as soon as she'd arrived. Small talk made her feel uneasy and crowds always seemed to pose the threat of stampedes or drunken brawls that she could potentially get hurt in. What's worse was that every time she'd give in and head out to a social event, she would drink too much to help her feel a little calmer and wake the following day with a throbbing hangover. The sad thing in that case was that the only thing that could 'cure' her hangover was *kapana*, the acquisition of which would require her to put herself in the midst of yet another overcrowded social setting.

'Actually, I'll be studying this weekend. I need to nail my Theatre Studies theory so I really can't afford to be partying. Besides, I'll probably be such a buzz kill – I never really know how to act at those things. I'd much rather be indoors, where I'll be comfy-cosy. Thanks for the invite though.'

INamgu was right. She was known to be extremely antisocial. She hated large crowds and strangers and she could not hide it. Besides, she preferred to keep her friendship with Sophia to herself. The company of good music and a good book was far more appealing to her than a party.

'Oh no you don't, I'm dragging you along and I'm not taking no for an answer.' Sophia was always concerned that ǀNamgu wasn't living a well-balanced life and she wanted her to get out more, especially to get time away from Tangeni.

'Great, then it's settled. I'll see you both tomorrow night.' As she walked away, Khoënhoandias blew air kisses in their direction, shining her pearly white teeth at them.

On their way home, Sophia told ǀNamgu about all the flirting she and Khoënhoandias had been indulging in and how she had started developing real feelings for her.

Nine

The party started out like any other raging banger: dimmed lights, people with frenzied looks in their eyes sprawled around the mansion, some dancing, some indulging in recreational drugs, most drinking, some kissing with their bodies pressed up against each other. Some were already passed out on the black leather couches in the lounge, while others were in the back yard playing dominos, talking, laughing and drinking way too much. The air was buzzing with a cocktail of trap, hip hop and house music meshed with chatter and laughter. Exams were about to start and everybody was desperate to blow off some pent up steam that had built up during the final semester.

Sophia worked the room like she owned the place. She was completely in her comfort zone, a social butterfly, talking, drinking and flirting her way around the room with a socially anxious and uncomfortable INamgu following closely behind. INamgu's discomfort wasn't only caused by her disdain for social settings, the fact that the music rang excruciatingly loud in her ears (so much so, that she couldn't hear herself think) but also because of the fact that she was dressed in clothing that wasn't hers. Sophia had talked her into wearing an outfit that she'd picked out from her wardrobe after nagging ǀNamgu that her clothes were too reserved and boring for a party. She had dressed ǀNamgu in a black leather skirt, a black tightly fitted tank top, a lengthy cotton cardigan that lightly grazed the black ankle boots that ǀNamgu already owned. As they circled the room, ǀNamgu kept tugging at the skirt she wore in an effort to lengthen it. Eventually they ran into Khoënhoandias.

'You made it! You look amazing, both of you. Wow ǀNamgu, you switched up your style! I love it. Have you guys had anything to drink yet? Come, what's your poison, we have vodka and beer, what can I get you? Personally I love me some vodka. Beer just isn't for me, I can't stand the taste and smell; honestly, I don't know how people stomach the stuff. I'm having vodka with cranberry juice as a mixer. I'm sure you guys will enjoy it too.'

Before either Sophia or ǀNamgu could get a word in, Khoënhoandias was already pouring them mixtures of vodka and cranberry juice and shoving the drinks into their hands.

'You two need to catch up, cheers!' She toasted. The two friends raised their white Styrofoam cups at her and gulped up their drinks.

'Thanks, that's actually really yummy, not as bad as I expected it to be.' ǀNamgu wiped her mouth and handed an empty cup back to Khoënhoandias who poured yet another of the vodka mixture, filling up their cups.

'You look really great! I love seeing you outside the theatre.' Sophia hadn't taken her eyes off Khoënhoandias.

'And I love seeing you outside your clothes,' Khoënhoandias winked at Sophia and they both giggled.

'Let's not babysit these drinks. Cheers to looking great both outside the theatre and outside our clothes, oh and to getting out.' They toasted once more and Khoënhoandias poured them yet another round of drinks.

'I thought you would've forgotten what I look like naked by now. It's been a while. You kinda went AWOL on me,' Sophia fiddled with her hair.

'I could never forget a goddess, Sophia. I think I just got a little scared, because I know you don't commit and I'm not really into casual flings, so, yeah, I kinda ghosted but I probably should've said that back then.' Khoënhoandias looked up at Sophia from the drinks she was pouring, 'You do know how sorry I am, don't you?' She handed the drinks over to Sophia and |Namgu.

'Gee, thanks for remembering that I'm here,' |Namgu mumbled under her breath as she downed her drink and went on to pour herself another.

'Huh?' Sophia furrowed.

'Nothing, don't mind me,' |Namgu retorted in a whisper.

'Yeah, of course I know,' Sophia replied to Khoënhoandias, 'you did send me all those texts apologising but it's nice to get an explanation too. No harm, no foul, you were protecting your peace, I get that, but you didn't need to. I actually *like you*, like you.'

|Namgu was bored and annoyed with the other two for leaving her out of their conversation so she wandered around the house cloudy with cigarette and hookah smoke that seemed to suck the air out; there was no air to breathe, and she kept bumping into backs and shoulders, and getting her feet stepped on by one too many strangers.

It was when she reached the bathroom and looked at her reflection that she realised just how drunk she was. The room was spinning so she splashed some water onto her face and the eyeliner and mascara that Sophia had applied for her earlier on, ran down her cheeks. She wiped her face on a white hand towel and left it lying on the floor smudged with makeup stains as she shut the bathroom door behind her and set out to find Sophia again.

Swallowed up by the crowd, Namgu was thrown into a state of drunken panic which fed her anxiety. She decided that she had had enough of the party and that it was time to go home. She stumbled around, colliding with more strangers; their fuzzy looking dancing bodies and the pale faced figure slouched on a couch amidst others made her even more dizzy while a familiar chill ran down her spine making the room spin faster and the music even more incoherent. She wanted to, or rather, needed to vomit. *Not in here*, she thought to herself as she took a deep breath in and pushed her way out to the back yard which most people had vacated because as the night grew older, the air had grown colder.

She stumbled her way to the far end of the backyard and as her thoughts spiralled out of control, her stomach did two back flips and a force made its way up through her guts, bringing a great lump to her throat and then a stream of foul smelling chunks of puke came pouring out of her mouth as her eyes watered. The loud music, chatter and laughter was almost out of earshot now and she was out of eyesight, or at least she hoped so. When it was all out of her system, she sat down on a rock, as carefully as a drunk person could and contemplated just how much she'd had to drink, but smiled to herself at the thought of having let loose and just stepped outside her comfort zone for the night. She used her right forearm to wipe her mouth clean, the smell of smoke lingering on her clothes. *Never again*, she thought.

She turned her head as she heard the sound of crushed twigs amongst the rustling of leaves. A tall, ghost-faced, shadowy figure was walking in her direction.

'You got sick, *nê*, I saw that *deurmekaar* look in your eyes. I wanted to bring you this *pani* and make sure you're okay.' ǀNamgu recognised Thomas, her classmate in psychology, by his deep, clear voice that had most of her female classmates swooning. He stood hovering above her with a bottle of water in his hand.

'Hey, thanks so much.'

She used the first few gulps to rinse out her mouth and then drank without pausing for air until the bottle in her hands was empty.

'*Jirre* that smells like piss man, let's walk further down, away from the noise and that stink. I'm sure you don't want people to see you like this. I'll sit and talk to you until you feel better *nê*?'

A pale, muscular hand reached down and helped her up, draped her arm around his neck and walked her further away from the voices and possibly eyes peering at them through the long sliding glass door that opened up to the backyard. They walked a distance and found some rocks to sit on.

'You looked really out of place tonight – I was shocked to see you at a party like this.' Thomas eyed ǀNamgu who had turned him down more than once. He draped his jacket over her shoulders and shifted himself closer to her. ǀNamgu was truly grateful for the bottled water but she was very tired and she did not want to make small talk with a man that she had no interest in. All she wanted to do was go home. She removed his jacket and handed it back to him.

'Thanks, Thomas, I really needed that water. You're a life saver, and I wish I could stay and chat with you, but I really need to find Sophia so we can make our way home now. I just want my bed.'

She started to get up but the man seated on the rock beside her firmly placed his fingers around her tiny bicep and pulled her down. He didn't want her to leave. This was his opportunity to make a move on her outside of campus.

'Don't be rude ǀNamgu. I just did you a big favour and you still act like I don't deserve to be in your presence. *Jy hou vir jou altyd warm as ons in die klas is omdat jy slim is*, well we're not at uni right now. I know you want me and you know that I want you. You just want us to keep it a secret, right? Well, nobody's watching us right now. It'll be our secret. Just one kiss?' Thomas had a wild look in his eyes, a hungry look of insatiable thirst, lust and greed, a type of merciless aggression radiating from just the look on his face. She couldn't believe the change from his warm concern to the type of gluttony that drove men to colonize nations, seizing land and raping resources without regret or remorse.

Before ǀNamgu could even think or breathe or move, the man beside her went from friend to foe; in seemingly one swift move, he'd pulled her down to the ground so that her head landed on some twigs and sand and her legs folded quite oddly beneath her. He placed each of his hands around her ankles, just where her boots began and yanked down, pulling them in opposite directions. He lay down on top of her, reached down, unzipped his pants and let his erect penis emerge from his khaki trousers. He used two

80

fingers to pull her white cotton panties to the side, entered her forcefully and began to thrust violently, grunting in her ears, drooling all over her face and breathing heavily. He was saying things but |Namgu heard nothing, felt nothing.

|Namgu had left her body. She was floating somewhere among the tree branches looking on at her lifeless body, *speak, scream, say no, say no, say no, tell him to stop, tell him to get off, look there; nearby your hand, there's a rock over there – hit him over the head, bite him, scratch him, do something, anything.* Her mind was racing, her thoughts were putting up a fight, but all her body could do was shiver in response to the cold air and allow tears to flow from her eyes. There was no screaming or fighting or hitting him over the head with a rock, none of the struggle she'd read about in books and seen in rape scenes on television – just a dead, lifeless body whose only response was an endless fountain of tears. She watched with her mind's eye as he thrust harder and harder and faster and faster all the time, until one last hard thrust, a loud grunt, followed by a deafening silence.

Could nobody see her? How could she be so invisible, so alone, so unimportant, so socially awkward that nobody came after her? Not even Sophia, the one she trusted the most. She moved her eyes from side to side but there was no one, only her lifeless body and the monster on top of it.

'Thanks for making this so easy. You girls usually put up a fight, but you just lay there – I liked that.' He stood over her motionless body as he zipped up his pants and walked away crushing twigs and dead leaves beneath his feet as he did.

Move. He's gone now. MOVE. She willed herself to get onto her feet, and walked or stumbled, or crawled or floated – she didn't know – through the yard – she wasn't quite sure how she moved but she summoned all the strength left in her and made her way through the crowd, walked out through the front door, reached inside her top, under her bra and pulled out her phone.

The last dialled number was Tangeni's. She pressed the call button and a sleepy Tangeni answered the phone. She sobbed into the phone. She could barely get a word out but Tangeni knew that she was in trouble and she'd told him where she'd be. 'I'm coming to get you. Wait outside,' he said, fully awake, very worried and a little annoyed. *What now?* Tangeni was pulling on sweatpants and squinting in the light that he'd turned on, looking for his car keys. *Jesus, I told her not to go, I warned her.* He drove off in the still of the night. The only things that were buzzing with light were the 24 hour takeaway joints, clubs and bars frequented by drunks, degenerates and delinquents at ungodly hours. *Lord forgive them for they know not what they do — wasting their God-given lives away, drinking and carrying on, turning the city into Sodom and Gomorrah. This is Babylon.* This is what he had spent so many hours trying to convince his peers about. When you're under the blood of Jesus, nothing can phase you, nobody can hurt you, because you walk by faith and not sight, and that walk almost never leads you toward debaucheries that could only lead to nothing but trouble, but they never understood. Nobody understood the love of the Lord like he did and thus nobody could comprehend the wrath that the Lord would most certainly bring down upon any that strayed from Him. *My God is an angry God, Praise Him,* he thought as the music of the All Saints Choir Group rang softly through his car speakers.

He took two left turns and slowed down the car until it came to a complete stop.

He wasn't going to get out of the car and INamgu knew that – these types of spaces weren't good for the purity of the soul. He spotted her and watched her make her way to the car, crying, trembling from the cold, stumbling towards his car. She looked a mess. She pulled the silver handle, opened the front door, sat in the passenger's side, shut the door and wept, wailing as she did, leaning over to put her head on his chest.

'What happened? Was there a fight? Where's Sophia?' Tangeni had never seen her like this before. 'You're drunk – I can smell the booze and vomit on you. Jesus, what are you wearing?' He started to pick a few twigs from her hair with one hand as he used the other to hold her shoulder.

'He... he, he, raped me! And I didn't stop him, I... I, I couldn't stop him, c-c-couldn't breathe, couldn't move, I just let him, didn't even say no. It hurt so much, it still hurts....' She shook and sobbed uncontrollably now, violently even, stammering through her sentences, some of which made sense, others not, but Tangeni heard her loud and clear.

'I told you not to come here tonight, especially not wearing that; you're barely wearing any clothes. Were you flirting with this guy? Besides what you're wearing, what'd you do that made him think you wanted him? INamgu, you know that premarital sex is a sin. Going out of your way to tempt others is even worse. Jesus, I can't even look at you right now.' He removed her from his chest, pushed her to the side.

'Put your seatbelt on,' he snapped as he turned the key in the ignition, drove her home and put the car in park mode.

'This has gone on for long enough now INamgu. I put up with so many ungodly things for this relationship, and now this. What you did tonight is where I draw the line. We simply can't be together anymore.'

'But Tangeni, I… it wasn't… I didn't do anything, it was…'

'I can't put myself in sin's way for you any longer but I will pray for you every day, the way I always have.' He leaned over her and pushed her door open. As she got out of the car that now smelled of an infusion of booze and lemon air freshener, he sighed heavily, 'It's over, INamgu.'

She felt too weak to respond, sure that her knees would buckle beneath her if she stood there any longer. She watched as his silver hatchback sped off and disappeared into the night, leaving her standing there alone.

Ten

Thomas felt a sickening sense of accomplishment after what he'd done to ǀNamgu. He'd finally got what he'd always wanted. He found her to be a challenging conquest, so to him, he'd achieved the seemingly impossible and that made him feel like *The Man* that his friends had always talked him up to be. His friends had often told him that there wasn't a single woman who could resist him and they'd made fun of him whenever ǀNamgu turned down his advances, so he resolved to make it a point to brag about his monstrous act to them.

Thomas grew up in Sonop, a small town near Mariental, a town full of unpaved roads lined with shebeens and filled up with children whose feet were grey from playing street soccer with balls made from tattered plastic bags. He was raised by his grandmother and a single mother who barely had time for him because they were too busy working to make sure they could survive. He had never met his father and had been left to his own devices growing up. The principal at his school had a soft spot for children who came from low income and single parent households, and established a program that would offer regular extra classes to them. His principal always saw to it that there was at least one adult in these children's

85

lives who was looking out for them and encouraged them to stay in school and seek more for themselves, because it was not always possible for him to be present. Some of the boys in his program fell through the cracks, but others ended up matriculating, and one or two even went up to university level, like Thomas.

Without much adult supervision, Thomas learned most of what he knew about life, including pursuing women, from gangs of older boys who got up to nothing but trouble. He grew up believing that he could take whatever he wanted, even that which did not belong to him. The first 'lesson' he learned about women was dictated to him by Six, the leader of the gang of boys that he grew up with. Whenever he felt attracted to a woman, Six's words would ring in his ears, *'Meat is meat and man must eat!'*

The first time that Thomas raped a girl was when he was thirteen years old. He watched as Six and the others took turns raping a girl that he liked at the time. Her name was Adora. She had skin that resembled the desert dunes and puppy dog eyes that always appeared to glisten. She grew up in the same street as Thomas and their mothers worked for neighbouring Afrikaners in the same neighbourhood on the other side of the train tracks, so they walked to and from school together every day. On a Friday after school, they were forced to take a route that Thomas had been avoiding because he had been trying not to run into his friends along the way, but that day was different. Their usual route had been closed off due to construction so he didn't have any other choice.

'Awe Tom *en* Jerry, *kom gou hier.* I wanna so (show) you something!' Six and the others were kneeling over an elevated drain playing dominoes.

Thomas's heart sank but he knew that he couldn't refuse. The last time he had said no to Six, he and the rest of the gang took turns beating him up and then drove him to Hardap Dam in the middle of the night and left him stranded there; he knew better now. He tightened his grip on Adora's hand and they walked over to them.

'Game's over *ouens*! Let's go check out the *Spookhuis*. Thomas, who's your friend?' Six got up and wiped his hand on his trousers and held it out.

'Hello, I'm Adora,' Adora whispered in her husky voice, shaking his hand. Six pulled her close to him and started walking off to the abandoned house where homeless people would often go for shelter.

'Wait! Adora has to be home now, her mother is waiting for her. We should go… now,' Thomas was practically speed-walking after them.

'Don't lie Thomas, my mom is at work. What's with you?' Adora never liked it when people spoke for or over her. She was annoyed with Thomas and warming up to Six whom she'd heard about, was fascinated by, but had never got the chance to meet.

'You heard the lady,' Six snickered.

The abandoned house looked as abandoned as it was, with weeds and shrubs overgrowing what could have been a lawn, broken windows, and street art and swear words spray painted on its walls. The smell of stale cigarettes and dried up urine lingered in the air, joined by the smell of a newly lit cigarette on Six's blackened lips.

'*Speel daar vir ons musiek, jong!*' Six beckoned one of the other guys who only seemed to speak or make a move under Six's direct orders. The drums and bass of Maleisa music filled the room. Thomas felt helpless, but not desperate enough to try harder to get Adora out of what he knew was a dangerous situation. His cowardice turned to frustration. What could he do against the combined weight of Six and his gang? He truly believed that there was nothing he could do to help Adora now.

'Say, Adora, has Thomas ever kissed you? I know he likes you, I see the way he looks at you.' Six ran his fingers between her box braids as he passed the cigarette to one of the others.

Thomas's gut churned.

'Never,' she rolled her eyes, 'he's a bit… slow.'

Six sat down on the tattered mattress on the floor and patted the spot next to him.

'Come sit here by me, I'm not so slow.' Adora sat next to Six and they started kissing, slow and gentle at first and then harder and rougher.

Thomas started to his feet and shifted his hands around inside his pockets.

'Okay, that's enough, Thomas, please let's go home now,' Adora finally allowed her attention to drift from the notorious older boy to the actual danger that she might be in, but it was too late.

'It's enough when I say it's enough. Hold her down guys.' The other boys obeyed as Six loosened his pants.

Thomas stood frozen in fear and cowardice. Adora looked at him with pleading eyes.

There's no way out, we're outnumbered. Thomas frantically looked around the room. *Why didn't she listen to me before?* He frowned, wiping the sweat from his brow.

'Come here, Thomas, it's your turn.' Six got up, walked over to Thomas, and shoved him towards the mattress where

Adora lay crying, held down by the other boys, one of them cupping his hand over her mouth.

'No, I can't, she's my friend... please.' Thomas was crying too but Six didn't care.

'If you don't do it, I will make all of these filths fuck her too and I will make you watch, and when they are done, I will kill her myself!' The fear rose in Thomas's gut like an expired meal. He walked as slowly as he could, silently wishing that he could freeze time.

'I'm not joking, you know *mos*?' Six stood with his arms crossed and a demonic look in his eyes. Thomas believed him.

There's no escape. There's too many of them. His blood ran cold when he finally reached her. His hands shook like leaves in the wind about to detach from the safety of their tree. He could barely undo his pants as he softly said, 'I'm so sorry.' Adora only cried louder in response.

He lay down on top of her and clumsily shoved himself inside her, feeling a strange mix of pleasure, guilt and disgust. The others laughed and cheered him on but all he could do was swallow the impending vomit making its way up through his throat enough times for him to whisper a weak, 'Sorry' to Adora, but after a while, he found himself not feeling sorry. The pleasure he felt superseded his guilt and a sense of sickening power arose within him. He started to like the applause and cheers from the others, and something dark and evil awakened within him, something that he would carry with him for all his life.

Eleven

Namgu was beside herself with utter disbelief over what had happened to her. What Tangeni had just said, how he had just abandoned her, that didn't matter, he didn't matter. What Thomas had done had ended her, nothing could or would ever be worse than that. She cried and cried and cried in anguish and pain that all the tears in all the world could not wash away. Her mind was like a darkened circus, her thoughts racing, prancing with flashbacks and replays, with sounds of his breath ringing in her ears. The what-ifs and if-onlys came pouring in like hail in a blizzard. She questioned her every action, every moment that led up to her rape.

How could this have happened to me, she thought, *what did I do that made this man think that I wanted him, that I wanted this? Why couldn't I fight? Why did I just lie there? Why didn't I scratch him, or bite him or grab that rock and hit him over the head with it? Why didn't I defend myself, protect the virginity that I fought so hard to maintain? Why on earth or any other planet didn't I scream or cry for help? Surely someone would've heard me, and come to my rescue? I could've stopped him, but I didn't. I deserved it.*

The affirmation made her hate herself even more than she hated him. That man had ripped her soul apart, and she had let him. It was as though her consciousness had left her and was watching from a safe distance while the wicked beast violated and had his way with her body. She thought herself a coward, a weakling, deserving what had happened to her. *My fault, shouldn't have been there, shouldn't have worn these.*

The thoughts came pouring down like rain during a flood up north. Rain that swallowed up everything in its reach and didn't care much for the houses where mothers breastfed their young or fathers worked in the fields to provide for their families or children played in the mahangu fields. A flood that only brought pain and anguish, a flood that only brought with it death and destruction. How the world had lied to her: *You are more likely to be raped by someone that you know and trust, a friend or family member.* She had read that somewhere. *What about the rest then? Are they to be excused, to live in the shadows forever? You are more likely to be raped by a rapist, she thought… A rapist can be anyone, friend or foe, gentlemen or misogynist, anybody can rape you at any time, at any place, even in the back yard of a mansion full of people that you've been attending classes with every day and guess what? Nothing changes, the party goes on, the music never stops playing, your peers keep on dancing, the drinks keep flowing as though your insides were intact, as though the whole world hadn't cracked right down the middle and split you in half; life went on. Life went on for everyone but the victim. The victim dies. She dies and nobody knows. I can't breathe or eat or think or move. I am drowning while the rest swim and splash happily, but not me, never me, so I have no other choice but to succumb to my untimely death. I must go because death is calling me and I am already dead so I must obey its call.*

She moved as though she were in a trance, in slow motion, like a soulless entity, floating about. The tears kept flowing down her face like a raging sea hungry to swallow up the face that they covered and her body shook violently as she walked over to the medicine cabinet in the bathroom. Everything from prescription painkillers, sleeping pills, to the cough syrups she'd often scold Sophia to keep refrigerated, to antihistamines that they both used to fend off sinus attacks stood facing her. She sprawled them all out across the dressing table and the display resembled something that you might see in a candy shop. She grabbed a handful, popped them in her mouth and swallowed hard. She could feel some of them scraping the edges of her oesophagus, all the way into her belly, and she repeated this action, until the dressing table was clear, running to the basin to wash down the drug cocktail using the cough syrup and tap water.

This is the only way, she thought, as images of his face flashed across her mind. The darkened circus of thoughts and what-ifs and if-onlys would haunt her forever, unless she put an end to it now. She didn't fight him off before but she would stop him from haunting her now and forever. Yes, death was the answer, she was sure of it – the dead don't have heart beats or blood flow or brain activity which meant that dead people couldn't think or feel or remember, and she didn't want to think or feel or remember, so this was inarguably the only way out, her only escape.

Her friends and family would miss her, *would they*? But they'd get over it, they'd go through all the necessary stages of grief – denial, anger, bargaining, sadness and acceptance – and that would be that, life would go on. Life always goes on. She knew that because even as she was being raped, the party had continued, and even as Tangeni drove her home, shattering what was left of her soul even more with his words, traffic went by. People had places to go, other people to see. Life would go on, just as it always had. The clock never stops ticking, the hands of time cannot be turned back, nothing could undo what had been done to her, but she could escape it and death was the carriageway that would lead her to eternal peace.

She took off all Sophia's clothes and let them fall to the floor beside her bed. She slid open the bedside drawer and held a silver switchblade that she so often used for various DIY arts and crafts projects, firmly in her hands. Her body had stopped shaking and trembling from her weeping now. She got up and floated toward the bathroom again. Her head felt heavy and her thoughts became jumbled up so that they no longer made sense. Black blotches and circles appeared before her eyes. Her whole body felt heavy. She turned on the two faucets, stepped in the shower and propped herself up against the wall. Usually she would have had a problem with being seated on the shower floor, but germs were another one of the things she would no longer have to worry about. She lifted the blade with her right hand, slid it upwards, pressing it hard against her left wrist, just below her palm and slid the blade forcefully into her skin, making a straight cut from one side to the other, from which blood began to flow. *Shit. Vertical, not horizontal,* but it was too late. Her body slouched to the side, her head hitting the floor as it landed. A mixture of blood and water swirled around her motionless body and in her mind the circus had been shut down and darkness ensued.

Twelve

'Another drink?' Sophia held out her hand, the lights were low and the tempo of the music decreased.

'Of course,' Khoënhoandias handed Sophia her empty cup.

'To us reuniting and hopefully not parting any time soon.' Sophia felt a tinge of regret at her unintended vulnerability but she felt somewhat grounded and safe in Khoënhoandias' presence. Saying stuff like that didn't come easy to her, but it felt right and she knew that it wasn't just the alcohol talking.

'I'll drink to that.' They toasted as the tempo of the music quickened again, 'Dance with me?' Khoënhoandias asked with a lingering look in her eyes.

'Let's!' Sophia took her hand and led her to the centre of the room, held her by the waist and they seemed to sway to their own beat, basking in the electric vibrations in the air around them. The vibrant aura around them was magnetic and almost everyone around them stared and marvelled at the way they danced, kissed and caressed each other. They got lost in each other so much that they lost track of time. It was well past midnight when the pair decided to leave the party and spend the night together.

'Shouldn't we find |Namgu? Tell her we're leaving?' Khoënhoandias took Sophia's hand as they made their way to the front door, both of them scanning the rooms they passed for any sign of |Namgu.

'If I know her, and I do, then I'd confidently say that she's called Tangeni to pick her up. She's probably fast asleep in bed by now. Here, I'll text her.' *Hey hun, thanks for coming out tonight, going home with Khoendi, please thank Tangeni for getting you home safely for me, xo.* The text was typed and sent in a matter of seconds and the pair drove to Khoendi's flat in Klein Windhoek where she lived alone. Her parents were diplomats and moved from country to country every four years or so, and they had set up their daughter in what they deemed to be the safest area in the city. Her townhouse was in one of those fancy gated communities, with 24 hour security, access codes, the works.

They drove down after passing through the security gate, past the park and pool area to Khoendi's house. Khoendi pulled up the hand break and brought her car to a stand-still in her garage. She looked over at Sophia, took her wild mess of curls into her hands and pulled her close. They sat and kissed in the car, getting lost between time and space. After eons, they pulled away from each other and hurried out of the car. Khoendi led Sophia in through the spacious open plan living area, up the stairs and into her bedroom.

When they made love, it was as though time stood still. In that moment, all the pleasurable experiences in existence came together inside and between them as their bodies entwined. Making love felt like swimming in the ocean, the waves crashing in on them and pulling them into all its majesty. Like lying underneath the sky and gazing at the moon and stars, breathless at the sky's infinite beauty. It was like a mountain's view of a thousand sunsets and sunrises. And in those thousands of moments there in Sophia's warm embrace, Khoendi felt safe and the love that burned in Sophia's eyes made her forget all her loneliness. They fell asleep in each other's arms, forgetting the world around them.

After enjoying a hearty breakfast prepared by Khoendi, they drove over to Sophia and |Namgu's place, enjoying the stillness that most mornings brought along during the weekend.

'Honey, I'm home,' Sophia giggled, as she called out to |Namgu.

'She's usually getting lost in some psych book or other by this time, or fast asleep. Shame, maybe she's a little hungover. I'm going to see if she needs me to pick up *kapana* or something. Just get comfy! You've been here before, grab a book, and slouch on a bean bag.' Khoendi did just that.

'A little hungover! Are you kidding me? She probably looks and feels like death warmed up. She's not a drinker and she had way too many last night.' Sophia laughed as she made her way to |Namgu's bedroom. She didn't knock; she never did. |Namgu's bedroom was a hot mess. Sophia found the empty packets of pill containers, the open drawer, plops and blotches of blood, drops of water dripping from the faucet in the bathroom. *What the fuck.* Flashes of her mother's dead body violently slain, projected themselves onto the screen of her mind. She was six at the time and it was on the news. She wasn't new to seeing the blood of a loved one. *Where is it? Where is her body?* Sophia thought as she paced around the room looking for more blood and her friend's body. She searched frantically from room to room, desperately hoping and praying that she hadn't been too late. *Where is she?*

Thirteen

'I just don't understand… Why would such a beautiful girl do something like this? And so young! Shame. You know some people just can't cope with it. Poor thing. *Aai,* but did you see what the paramedics said she must have been wearing before they found her? I don't understand why young girls leave their houses dressed like that. You know our men can't control themselves. They aren't used to such things, and we women should know better. I mean, you open the newspapers every day, and what do you see? Never-ending rape cases being reported.'

The short, tubby nurse was busy checking the file that lay next to the bed that |Namgu was in while the other followed her closely, nodding and agreeing with everything she said but never offering an opinion of her own.

'She can hear you, you insensitive, ignorant, witch!' Hotani stormed into the room and dialled the number belonging to Dr Paul.

'Dr Paul, this is Hotani. I've just walked in on two nurses on duty to care for my sister, and I would like to request – no – *insist* that they be removed immediately. My parents are spending thousands for her to receive the best psychiatric care here at your facility, and their treatment of her is unacceptable. Please see to it that they are replaced as a matter of urgency. Good day.'

And with one swift move, she hung up and waved the two nurses out of the room. Sometimes the patriarchy made a home for itself in the minds of the women it was structured against. *But no talk like that near my sister.* She paused and watched |Namgu carefully as she walked over to her.

It seemed her entire life played out in her mind. From the moment that her baby sister had been born, she had been intent on one-upping her. First she had a point to prove because she knew how badly her father had wanted a boy child and people, especially fathers, have very high expectations of their sons. In order to live up to this expectation – it suddenly struck her, this *assumed* expectation – her life had revolved around pleasing her parents and doing everything according to their advice and instruction.

|Namgu was right. I do everything that mom and dad want me to. I even dress the way ti ma *does. My good grades were never for me but to please them, even my career is tailored to their liking; ti Elotse!* A red hot fire burned away at her heart – guilt, an indescribable force that would probably haunt her until her dying day. She drew a long shaky breath, holding her hand to her heart. *|Namgu? Suicide…? I would never have thought; she's so brave and fearless. That pain must've cut really deep.* But that's the thing with suicide, it doesn't stop the pain, shame or guilt, but merely passes it on from one person to the other.

The people left behind are the ones racked with guilt and the one who attempts suicide pays the ultimate price for their inner demons and depression.

'ǂNamgu, *ousies ke*, I know you're awake my love. I'm so sorry that you had to hear all that. How are you feeling today? You're recovering so very well, you're so strong. We've been taking turns coming in to visit you. Mom and dad left while you were asleep – I had to force them to leave, they've wanted to be by your side this entire time. Look, I know it's difficult and I know you must be scared but, please, just tell us who… who raped you. We need to find him, we need to get justice for you.'

ǂNamgu was squinting up at Hotani, allowing her eyes to adapt to the light and studying the foreign room that she was in. She raised her arm to find that it was tightly wrapped in bandages where she had cut herself; in the other arm she found a see-through tube with a cloudy liquid running through it connected to a bag hanging from a metal stand on wheels.

'I don't want justice, I want peace. Why didn't you guys just leave me, why didn't you guys just let me die?' ǂNamgu raised her voice tremulously, half sitting up, half lying down, breathing heavily and tugging at the tube inserted into her arm. She felt as though her body had betrayed her, deceived her – how insolent. Like a television set or radio player that refused to obey the commands given to it by its owner. Her body had failed to give her the peace that her mind and heart so desperately cried for. A nurse entered the room and administered a shot into ǂNamgu's drip, telling her that everything would be okay. The sedative began its work almost immediately and Hotani's sobs were the last thing she heard.

Over the following days, her mind forced her to relive the ordeal numerous times. He was on top of her again, pinning her down, his weight stopping her from breathing, his breath heavy in her ears, followed by the grunts, his thrusting, his voice, the mad look in his eyes, her body motionless, and the dirt in her hair. She woke up from the dreams screaming and crying so loud that her shrieks could be heard echoing through the centre. She was pulling off her bandages and yanking out her drip again, kicking off her blankets violently when the nurse would rush in and give her yet another sedative while stroking her hair and humming a soothing melody to her. Silence and darkness followed once more.

Fourteen

Her parents were informed by Dr Paul, that ǀNamgu would have to be admitted to the Mental Health Wellness Centre for a lengthened stay to receive intensive therapy and possibly medication to help her come to terms with her rape and the failed suicide attempt that had followed. Dr Paul also told them that she was bound by confidentiality and could not inform them of the goings-on during her therapy sessions with their daughter.

Dr Paul was one of the most renowned psychologists in the country. She was also one of the youngest psychologists to own a mental health care centre. Hers was the go-to facility for all types of social and psychological issues, from drug and alcohol addiction to anxiety and mood disorders, to other more severe cases such as suicidal patients and those with psychotic episodes and disorders.

Dr Paul had lived with Major Depressive Disorder for almost her whole life. She had been diagnosed at the age of thirteen when she had made her first suicide attempt. Prior to that, her parents had refused to have her see a psychologist, or any other mental health professional for that matter.

It was a very common belief amongst African parents that mental health illnesses were *'white people's illnesses'* and that those who claimed to suffer from them were merely attention seeking, spoiled liars, exaggerating their emotions and placing too much attention on their inner thoughts and emotions, attention which would have been better directed toward obtaining a good education in order ultimately to earn a good salary and raise a family, which according to them, would no doubt result in happiness.

She grew up as an only child, feeling extremely isolated and misunderstood, to the point where she had convinced herself that life was no longer worth living, that she didn't deserve to live. She felt unworthy, unheard and alone, and so on her thirteenth birthday she tried to hang herself using her school tie – all for nothing, because her mother had forgotten her office keys during lunch hour and had returned to find her daughter tying a loop around the old tree in the garden. Ever since then she had attempted suicide three more times before her parents sought out professional help for her, which happened to be even more shitty than the depression in itself, except for the medication that they had put her on. It was her shitty experience with shitty psychologists that made her want to become a not so shitty psychologist. She wanted to help people that were like her or worse, not that any mental illness or emotional disturbance should be minimalised in comparison to the next, but she still felt that she was one of the lucky ones, better off than someone stuck in a psychotic nightmare.

The worst cases for her were the psychotic disorders, the extreme hallucinations which plagued the patient with images, sounds and tactile irritations as well as delusions that tortured the patient with unrealistic beliefs of grandeur or extreme paranoia. Not to mention the lack of conscious awareness and complete disconnection from reality. Other extremes were the ones with compulsions so strong that made them scrub the skin off their hands from incessant washing because intrusive thoughts made them believe that their kid would die of some unspeakable illness if they didn't wash their hands fifty times a day, or something of the sorts; the ones whose depression drove them to suicide, the hard-to-reach, the incurables. She'd been taught throughout her studies that all psychological disorders could be managed, not cured, only managed and she truly believed and understood this even though she had fought against the notion during her undergraduate studies. She was young, impressionable, naïve, helplessly optimistic, unrealistically so, back then, but she understood now. Acceptance (both of the self and by another) and management were the closest things to cures when it came to psychological disorders.

ǀNamgu had recovered well enough from her wrist slash and attempted overdose in the hospital, and had come out of the coma after two weeks. Her parents had had her transferred directly to Dr Paul's Wellness Centre. Even though they thought a psychiatrist would be better suited for their daughter, they settled with Dr Paul because not only had she gone up to PhD level, but for the reputation that her wellness centre boasted. According to all their friends who were health professionals, she was their best bet. After a week of observation, strict suicide watch, and daily participation in the activities at the centre which included painting, role play, music lessons and journaling exercises, ǀNamgu seemed to be improving. Dr Paul used art therapy as a tool to help the patients relax and feel safe in their space. It made talk therapy easier because it gave the patients an opportunity to express themselves and their pain through art. It was fun, and they could let their guard down. By the start of the following week, Dr Paul decided that |Namgu was well enough to start therapy.

During their first session |Namgu was defensive and stand-offish.

'I know how this works. I've studied some of this stuff and let me tell you now, straight up, nothing's going to work unless you have a time machine. Do you own a time machine, Dr Paul? I don't think so. Can you un-rape me? Can you undo what that monster did to me? No. You can't, so it's safe to say that all the therapy in the world is not going to work on me, and, when the time is right, when you and your people and my family least expect it, or drop the ball, take your eyes off me for even just a split second, I'll do it again. And next time, I'll avoid dramatic goodbye texts, in the hopes of some salvation. I'll just do it and I won't stop until I am dead, do you hear me?' She was yelling, crying, pacing the room, never looking in Dr Paul's eyes, let alone in her direction.

'I hear you and you have every right to be as angry and hurt as you seem to be. What happened to you was terrible and nobody deserves that. I'm only here to try to help. I know that you know how all this works, so let's start with the basics. Is it safe to assume that you study at the University of Humanities? They're the only university here that offers psych. I did my undergrad there. I loved it.' She paused, carefully watching the young woman to see how her words were taken. 'So tell me what you know? You said you've studied some of this stuff. I'm assuming you're referring to the therapeutic process, yes?' There was a hint of light-heartedness at play in Dr Paul's voice.

'You know why I'm here. I'm here because something bad happened to me and so I tried to kill myself. Wow, what a revelation, can I go now?' Dr Paul watched |Namgu even more prudently, never taking her eyes off her. She watched every tear fall, she watched her pace and listened to her sobs and the content of her monologue quietly and carefully, and, when it was her turn to speak, she watched how her every word affected |Namgu.

|Namgu was taken aback by Dr Paul's cool, calm and collected way of being. She seemed unhurt by the attack on her profession and that infuriated her.

'So you have no comments or questions about what I just said? I just told you that I'm going to kill myself, AGAIN, and I might just do it right here in your so called *wellness* centre. How good would that be for business? Nobody would ever have a family member admitted here when I finally end my life here. Aren't you going to ask me how it makes me feel? You know, that generic line of questioning that they no doubt taught you in grad school.' Every word was an attack but the psychologist kept her tranquil composure, took a sip of her green tea and said, 'I hardly think the public would be so shocked. After all, this is a mental institution of sorts, something like that might well be expected. Anyway, tell me, what do you know about how this works? I'd love to hear if my old university is still as good as it was when I first enrolled or if it's fallen through the cracks like many other educational institutions.' Dr Paul was un-phased by |Namgu's intentional attacks on her or her centre. It was normal, part of the therapeutic process. The theorists referred to it as resistance and displacement and she expected it from most of her patients, especially the failed suicide attempts and those admitted by family members. The patient before her stopped pacing and stood with her back facing the psychologist staring at a painting of the ocean that was mounted on the wall.

'I'm tired. I'd like to go back to my room now. Thanks for your time Dr Paul but I can assure you that it's been wasted and will continue to be if you insist on more of these sessions with me.'

Traditionally therapy sessions run between forty five minutes to an hour. Only thirty minutes had passed, but Dr Paul decided that it was enough for the first session under the circumstances.

The past few days hadn't been kind to |Namgu and her decay was quite noticeable to anyone who laid eyes on her, even for a nanosecond. Her eyes were puffy and even though they appeared lifeless at first glance, a glimmer of hope could almost always be seen, by those who bothered to look intently. More telling was the hefty way she seemed to struggle to drag her entire being around, like a half-dead seal slithering upon a beach. She wore an oversized black turtleneck jersey and black leggings with bright pink slippers. Her feet lagged behind her, emitting a sound that felt like grinding teeth, as she made her way out to the garden. She was tired of talking, and she wanted to be outside, alone.

'It gets better.'

His voice broke her state of solitude. She was annoyed but when she managed to find his eyes, past the dreadlocks hanging loosely in his face, something inside her relaxed.

His eyes almost resembled her own, although the hope to lifeless ratio in his, outdid hers by far.

'We have different degrees of pain.' She watched him, as he lit the cigarette wedged between his fingers.

'They taking things from you, they take things they shouldn't,' a silver haired lady stood amongst the trees, almost perfectly at the centre of the garden yelling at the heavens. Nobody seemed to know what her real name was so they all just called her Angel, because she believed she could talk to God. Thousands believe that they can talk to God through prayer yet don't find themselves admitted to mental health facilities, because they speak to God in a way deemed appropriate in accordance with social agreements. Angel's prayers were always loud and public and frantic and incoherent.

|Namgu twisted her face as she watched the old lady repeatedly whisper a string of words to herself. She felt a pang of jealousy stir inside her; she longed for the lack of self-awareness and carefree nature with which psychotics navigated through life.

'Schizophrenia…' the boy blabbed, as he finger-combed his hair back and used the black rubber band from his wrist to tie up his hair, with the cigarette now held between his teeth. 'She's been here really long. All I've ever heard her say is stuff about people taking things that aren't theirs. Anyway, you're right, about pain. Even the schizophrenics, somewhere deep inside themselves, they feel it too, just like us, but in their own way.' He sighed heavily sending drifting shrouds of tobacco smoke out into the clear blue sky.

'I've heard about you… |Namgu, right?' He couldn't pronounce the click in her name and like most people, he didn't even attempt to say it right.

'It's ǀNAMGU. You press the tip of your tongue up against your two front teeth and suck the air between them. What've you heard about me?'

'Okay, ǀNamgu…' he did as instructed and managed to pronounce her name just right. 'Not much, just that there was someone else around my age here… We're the youngest at the moment, I think. It's a beautiful name. What does it mean?' He took a lingering drag from his cigarette, bending down to stump it out as he exhaled. He placed the leftover in his matchbox and the scent of an enmeshment of tobacco and cologne danced in the air around him.

'It means, "love each other"… Look… I came out here to be alone, do you mind?' There was something about him that made her want him to stay, but she wanted to be alone more than anything else.

'THEY TAKE THINGS, I SAY. THEY TAKE THINGS THEY SHOULDN'T TAKE!' Angel was yelling again, but this time she was perched up in a tree with her head tilted back, as though screaming to the leaves dangling above her.

'She's so free…' They both laughed.

'She is. When I get out of here, I wanna live like that. Not schizophrenic or anything, but just, you know… free. I'm Tanaka by the way. I know how you feel. You want to be alone, but you need someone. I'm not saying I'm that someone, even though I could be, but just, I don't know. If you ever want to talk or watch Angel talk to God or the stars or the leaves, I wouldn't mind doing that with you. I'm a mess, but I'm here.'

She didn't know anything about him and if he was at the Centre like her, then he really was a mess, but so was she and that made her breathe easily. *No more pretending,* she thought.

'You have nowhere else to be but here Tanaka, but I hear you, thanks.' She watched as he walked off on legs that seemed to go on forever. That night she thought of nothing but his hazel brown eyes glimmering with hope and how he towered above her. He must be at least one point eight metres. She couldn't get the smell of his cologne mixed with the smell of tobacco and nicotine out of her nose, or forget that it had been the first time she'd laughed since her attack. She thought about Tanaka until the moment she fell asleep.

Days passed and the following therapy sessions went similarly to the first, with |Namgu yelling, pacing and crying, insisting that Dr Paul was wasting her time and generally pissing on the field of psychology. Eventually, |Namgu became less resistant and opened up more and more to Dr Paul about everything except for what had brought her there in the first place. She even signed the mandatory documents that agreed to her further stay at the facility, a formality that all patients admitted by family members had to undergo. It was part of the healing process because therapy can never work if the patient does not want to receive the help that they deserve. |Namgu felt a sense of fear at the realisation of just how much vulnerability therapy called for, yet, at the same time, a deep sense of relief washed over her. She felt relieved to have someone to share her burden with, someone who could possibly help her carry the weight of the pain that she felt could destroy her, and that gave her hope; something she thought she would never feel again.

Fifteen

'Tell me what happened to you. Say it out loud, |Namgu. I've
been watching you, carefully listening to every word you've
said during our sessions and you keep tip-toeing around it.
So say it, tell me what happened to you.'

They had been going back and forth for about an hour,
making the most progress they had since their first session.
Dr Paul had changed her approach from cool, calm and
collected to direct and confrontational. She had used client-
centred, unconditional positive regard and attentive listening
to establish a foundation and gain what little trust |Namgu
had left to give, but now it was time for the real work.
Being confrontational with patients was frowned upon
amongst many counsellors but it could be highly effective
and Dr Paul thought that it was often the only way to get
clients to open up: by cracking them open at the centre
and laying them on the couch; vulnerable, present, with
nowhere to run or hide.

She stripped |Namgu of all her resistance and defences and
finally |Namgu told her in detail exactly what had happened
the night that she was raped until the morning she woke
up in the hospital drifting in and out of consciousness, and

then finally here she was, while Dr Paul recorded the entire session. When INamgu was done, she cried into an African print throw pillow that she clung onto for dear life as she lay on the couch. When her crying quietened down, Dr Paul reached for the recorder and pressed the stop button.

'To answer your question – the one you asked during our first session together, I cannot 'un-rape' you and I do not own a time machine, nobody can – you know this. A terrible thing happened to you. You didn't deserve it, nobody does and the man that did it to you was wrong, a predator. Your anger, your pain, your sadness, even your wish to end your life is valid. You were raped and that is something that you're going to have to learn to live with for as long as you are alive. That man took your virginity, your trust, your right to have a say as to what you do with your body. Don't let him take your life too. He can't take your hopes, your dreams, your present and your future, the potential for happiness, the possibility to trust again, the calling to live again. Those are yours. Nobody can touch that part of you, and nobody can hurt that part of you or kill that part of you – only you, if you choose to. Or you can choose to live. You can choose to smile again, to heal, to nurture those dreams and aspirations, to run toward that dimmed light at the end of this treacherous tunnel, but only if you choose to and only if you do the work. Ever since we started these sessions, I've been saying one thing repeatedly; that awareness is the first step toward healing. A demon must always be called by its name before it is cast out.' She continued, 'You are ready, now, say it.'

'*HE RAPED ME! I WAS RAPED!*' INamgu shouted through the sea of tears streaming down her face, her voice growing louder and clearer all the time. Dr Paul waited for the moment that echoed with |Namgu's declaration to subside, picked up the recorder and handed it to her.

'This is a story. These are the words that make up a very painful memory, but that's all it is now, do you hear me? It's a story, a part of your life story, words, a memory. It's not happening right now. Look around you, look where you are – you are safe now. Put your left hand on your chest. Place your right hand on your belly.' |Namgu did as she was told.

'Breathe deep, just like we've been practising. You are yours |Namgu – no thing and no person can ever take you away from yourself and if they try to, like that man did, you hold onto yourself. You fight for yourself. You pick up the pieces and stand in your truth. You are wholly your own. Your body belongs to you, you belong to you, you are yours.'

Those last three words rang as silent whispers of hope in |Namgu's ears as she lay awake in bed that night staring at the tape recorder. What did Dr Paul expect her to do with it? She never said. She also didn't schedule their next session. Maybe she forgot and would inform one of the psychiatric nurses to let her know. *Jedi mind tricks*, she thought.

|Namgu felt lighter, like she could breathe with ease again, and for the first time since she'd been at the centre, she fell asleep without sedation and her dreams were free from nightmares. That night and the nights that followed, she dreamt of Sophia. They were laughing under an old crooked staircase and she looked happy again. Sleep was once more a safe space to venture into. One morning after breakfast she wandered into the gardens and took the sun for a full hour without any prompting from the staff at the Centre. She sat under an orange tree, watching ants pass

by her feet and looking at the arrangement of the colourful flowers spread around the garden.

She remembered her dream and thought about Sophia for most of the day, wondering why she hadn't been to visit her. She would have called Sophia but the Centre had a strict no-phone policy. *I'll ask to call her from Hotani's phone when she comes to visit again,* she thought as she sat soaking up the sun's rays emerging through the shade cast by the tree's branches. She'd pushed thoughts of Sophia out of her mind until this point because Sophia had become yet another painful reminder of all the things that she believed led to her rape, a reminder that she only now felt ready to face.

Suddenly her light was blocked by Tanaka's tall shadow, but she didn't mind because sometimes Namibia felt like it was a lot closer to the sun than the rest of the world.

'Hi…' He smiled, holding one hand behind his back.

'Hi…' She sat up, 'what are you hiding?'

'If you let me sit with you, I'll show you.'

'Ok, let's see.' She was curious. Her posture lengthened as she held out her hand, waiting for him to reveal whatever he was holding behind his back. He sat down next to her, close enough for his cologne tangled tobacco aroma to reach her, but far enough to respect her personal space.

In the two months that he'd been there, he'd learned that the mentally ill weren't big on touch or trust. Some were too paranoid to get close to or even talk to because they believed that the government was listening in on every conversation, or that their skin would fall off if anyone dared to touch them. Others only spoke to people that weren't really there, and most just wanted to be left alone, even though they needed somebody.

'It's a book I just finished reading... here.' He handed her the book and lit a cigarette.

'I know this one, lent my copy to a friend and haven't seen it since.' She leafed through the pages until she stopped on the page where the words, 'The Meaning of Suffering', caught her eye and left her feeling angry at the book and its author, so she shut the book and handed it back to Tanaka. 'Keep it.'

He exhaled as a trail of smoke floated up into the clouds. 'It's a good book, really great company, salvation disguised as literature.'

'Thank you.' She reluctantly took the book and placed it beside her. 'Why are you here?' The words came spilling out. She didn't mean to be so forward but something inside her made her want to know about Tanaka. She regretted her question immediately though, because he was most likely to ask her the exact same thing and she wasn't sure if she wanted him to know.

'So you're a straight shooter? That's refreshing. I have OCD, and not the type that people joke about when their friends appear to be neat-freaks. I'm the real deal. I have to touch all the doorknobs before leaving a building amongst other obsessive acts that basically made my life come to a standstill. Long story short, Dr Paul is a magician and I'm down to one doorknob. She thinks I'm ready for the real world and I'm ready to put this place in my rear view. I leave this evening.' He stumped out what was left of the cigarette on the sole of his shoe.

'Oh... I'm sorry... About the OCD... and I'm glad that you're getting out of here.' She wasn't, she wanted to know more about him. He seemed so carefree, so mellow, it was easy being near him.

'I wish I'd had the courage to talk to you sooner. I think we would've been great friends. Not that I'm saying we can't be friends outside of this place or anything. Maybe you don't even want to be friends but if you look on the last page of the book, you'll find my number written down there, you know, if you ever want to talk or... be friends.'

'Yeah, okay, sure. Aren't you going to ask me?'

'Ask you what?'

'Why I'm here...'

'I get the feeling that you'll tell me when you're ready. Before people come here, they've been through the worst and when we get here we're kind of forced to relive the worst every day, in therapy or in our dreams or sometimes through the reflections of ourselves that we see in each other. Sometimes it's just refreshing to not talk about it all the time, so consider this, me giving you a break, until you're ready.'

He wondered if he would ever see her or hear from her again and that evening as he stared at the Centre's gates through the rear view mirror of the city shuttle, he kicked himself for not taking her number.

Sometimes goodbyes are just goodbyes.

Sixteen

'Please, I'm begging you. Please, just tell me where she is? I need to see her. I have to be there for her. I'm just trying to understand. I... I don't get it, she was fine, we were fine. What happened to her? Why will nobody talk to me? Please Hotani, talk to your parents.' Sophia had been trying to get hold of ǀNamgu since the day after the party when she found her blood spilt. She'd mostly been showing up at Hotani's office, trying to convince her to convince her parents to let her see ǀNamgu, all to no avail.

'I get where you're coming from, but we just don't think it's for the best. Look, I didn't want to say anything before but my parents just don't think you're good for ǀNamgu; according to them, you've never been a good influence. People like you have no morals, no values, no religion, no God, what type of comfort could you possibly offer her?' Hotani had always been jealous of the relationship that Sophia had managed to forge with her sister. It was the type of connection that she longed to have with her sister, especially now, but never quite knew how to reach. She looked into Sophia's eyes and almost instantly regretted her cold words towards her, but it was too late. She knew Sophia wouldn't take it in silence and she was right.

'Really? You're bringing religion into this? Religion does not define character, nor does it determine the quality of friendship, or support, or love that one has to give. Look at Tangeni. Where is he now? With all the world's Christianity flowing through his veins, he seems to have abandoned your sister in her darkest hour and here I am, a heathen, as you would have it, begging insistently to be granted access to someone whom I love more like a sister and you deny me because my morals and values don't match yours, because I choose to live my life on my own terms, because I don't seek the approval of others in order to maximise my happiness as it so pleases me? Tell me, honestly now, Hotani, do you really believe, in your heart of hearts, that |Namgu does not want to see me, to talk to me or to be with me right now? Remember you can lie to me, but the truth will haunt you forever and you know it.' Sophia knew a dead cause when she saw it. She turned on her heel and started for the door.

A wave of hot shame broke over Hotani. She realised she couldn't allow her jealousy or judgement of Sophia to stand in the way of true friendship any longer. She would make her parents understand. She knew they would be up in arms about her sudden change of heart, but she would explain everything to them. Since she was a little girl she had followed her parent's orders down to the letter. She had a deep desire to please them and she sought out their applause, even at the expense of her relationship with her baby sister, but it was a price she had been willing to pay to be the apple of her parents' eyes. She would often plant ideas in their minds about |Namgu, how her life choices were disrespectful, how troubled she was, what a failure she was, the bad name she gave the family, anything bad that could be said about her sister, she had said. She had left no stone unturned in her mission to be the favourite, the star of the family. Shame flooded her, deep regret left her feeling shaky. Sophia didn't even know what had happened to INamgu. In spite of her numerous enquiries, none of the family would speak to her.

Her way of being had become clearer through recent discussions with INamgu who had read up on an Austrian psychiatrist, Alfred Adler. Adler asserted that first born children were prone to perfectionism at all costs. He further stated that first born children have a strong need for affirmation. He attributed their behaviour to overcompensation because of the threat of younger siblings' potential to rob them of undivided parental attention and affection. Most first born children become adults who work their whole life to gain back that lost attention and affection.

Lately, trying to be perfect was taking its toll on her. She had grown tired of it, and in light of what had transpired over the past weeks, she looked back at her contempt and envy of her sister with regret, and decided that it was time to give it up.

I don't always have to do what mom and dad think is right. For once, today, I can actually do what feels right to me...

'Wait! Sofia! You're right. I'm sorry, I'll take you to her. It's an hour's drive. Are you free right now? I just need to file a few documents and we can leave together.'

They drove in silence in the direction of Daan Viljoen, first through the city outskirts where thousands of shacks shone under the sun of poverty, the divide between the rich

119

and poor growing more and more evident as they drove from central Windhoek, past Hochland Park, towards Rocky Crest, Otjomuise, and past the roadblock. The way the city and Namibia in general was set up, was an astounding mix of intense poverty of the masses, coupled with dazzling wealth in the hands of very few. The latter had been acquired by means of apartheid under the guise of generational wealth and privilege. The former was a result of a system backed by years of mental, physical and financial oppression.

The road was long and mountains hugged it along both edges covered in various shrubs and thorny trees. Some trees had anthills for trunks and others were simply made up of thorns. What fascinated Sophia most about the land was that it always seemed to give more than what was expected of it. What was on the surface simply misrepresented what lay beneath. The land looked barren and unable to provide anything or anybody with the means to survive, but it did. The land hid boreholes and thick medicinal roots and fruits that provided its inhabitants with nourishment and the ability not only to survive, but also to thrive.

She thought about |Namgu and felt a mysterious sense of peace in the thought that no matter what had happened to her, she would get through it. Her friend was like a well of resilience and strength. She could survive anything, or at least, that is what Sophia wanted to believe. But what had happened? Why would none of them speak about it? None of them would talk to her. They took a left turn onto the gravel road and drove for about an hour until they reached a large black gate with the words Mental Health and Wellness Centre engraved in a board across the top of it. Hotani spoke briefly to the security guard, signed some papers then proceeded to drive in. A series of succulent plants and cacti pathed out the driveway, some of them sprouting flowers in a variety of colours, leading up to the bricked building that stood tall and wide before them. They parked the car and made their way in through the entrance, stopping at the reception area to sign in and have Sophia's name put onto the approved visitors list. Sophia was nervous, scared and worried to see her friend. She didn't know what state she would be in. She had no idea why she had tried to end her life – a fight with Tangeni perhaps? She was confused. The entire ordeal had shaken her to her core. The flashes of the bloody scene that she came home to the day after the party mingled with images of her mother's dead body in her dreams. They were all she could think about. She had barely eaten and wouldn't have got through her exams if it hadn't been for Khoënhoandias who had been a pillar of strength for her and whom she had grown quite attached to over the past few weeks, in fact, she had fallen in love with her, but not even the strength of their love could fill the |Namgu-shaped hole that tore through her heart. The receptionist led the way to the visitor's room which was brightly coloured with the windows as tall and wide as the walls and a thousand leafy green plants placed upon the window sills.

Dr Paul was very deliberate with the interior decorating as well as the landscaping in the garden of the Centre. She believed in the healing powers of light and plants, of nature in general which was partly why she had chosen the outskirts of the city for the Centre's location. She felt a strong need for people to get out of the hustle and bustle of the city, to retreat into nature for restoration and relaxation, in a space

121

where they could place all their energies into themselves and their healing. She believed that because flora had a direct, intensive and intricate interaction with the source of all life – the sun's light energy – the plants, trees and flowers radiated that light energy which promotes healing, and which is why she wanted her centre to be submerged in nature both inside and outside.

It was ǀNamgu's turn to water the plants in the visitor's lounge, a task which she'd grown to love and appreciate. Routine was important, self-care was important and this included not only the self as its own entity but also the space in which it existed. This type of narrative was often repeated during therapy with Dr Paul. ǀNamgu still hadn't heard back from her. *I'll enquire at reception after watering the plants*, she told herself. The water from the canister leaked into the pot plant but was overflowing and dripped onto the floor which she only noticed when she heard a familiar voice call her name. She shook her head and turned to see Sophia and Hotani waving at her from across the room. She opened her hand and the water canister fell to the floor. She marched over to them, wrapped her arms around Sophia to embrace her, 'I've missed you but I'm so damn mad at you!' and then drew back and shook her as warm tears fell from her face.

'How could you? How could you leave me like that? You invited me, you took me to that fucking party and then you forgot all about me so that you could run off and go play out your stupid bi-curious fantasies. And do you know where I was? Do you even care? Did I even cross your mind for one split second?' Her voice broke in a violent, distressed tenor that filled the room with the anger and agony that moved within her.

Everyone was staring now and those deemed to be out of their minds began cheering and laughing, celebrating the confrontation. Sophia was crying too.

'They takes things. They takes things they shouldn't.' Angel was there too.

'ǀNamgu, I… I don't understand. I knew you were hurt but they wouldn't tell me where you were. I missed you so much. I was so worried. I wanted to be here for you. I hope you know that! I'm sorry, I'm so sorry, I got so caught up and I just assumed that you'd phoned Tangeni to pick you up. I thought you were okay, please, I'm so sorry.' Sophia had no idea as to what her apology was for but she meant it, every part of her was sorry, because she could see the pain and rage emanating from ǀNamgu's eyes and vibrating in her voice.

'Let me fill you in, you self-involved twat, while you were having the time of your life at the party that you practically dragged me to, I was being raped, outside, in the fucking sand, in the fucking sand, Sophia! You got me drunk and abandoned me. Who the fuck does that? You're my best friend, you were supposed to have my back. The way I have yours, the way I've always had yours. How many times have I been there for you, taken care of you while you were piss drunk, made sure you got home safely, have been worried sick because I didn't want some random guy taking advantage of you, defended you whenever someone opened up their mouth to shame or disrespect you, even my own family? And in the end it was you. You who walked me into my darkest hour, you who led me to my moment of despair, you who dressed me in your whorish clothing, fed me alcohol that I never drink and then left me for dead.

What are you even doing here? I don't want you here. I don't want you near me.' Every word was like a series of slaps in the face. They hit hard and they cut deep.

'|Namgu, please, I didn't know. I mean, I knew you were hurt but I didn't know how, or why; if I had, I would've helped. Please, I'm sorry. I've been out of my mind with worry since I went back to the flat after the party and found it in such a state.'

|Namgu didn't want to hear it. All thoughts of feeling safe and secure under the staircase had vanished. She meant every word she said and all she wanted right then was to live in a world where Sophia didn't exist.

'LEAVE. Get out. Go!' she yelled, and with that she turned on her heels and stormed out toward her room. Hotani and Sophia walked to the car and drove back into the city in silence, with only the sound of Sophia's soft sobs filling the space between them.

Seventeen

'Where is she? Call her! Please. I need to see her now.'
Like everyone else within good distance of the visitor's
lounge, the receptionist had heard every word of |Namgu's
confrontation with Sophia. She had the good sense to call
Dr Paul in for an emergency appointment, something that
wasn't uncommon in the Centre.

Dr Paul was there within the hour. Emergency sessions
were a regular thing in her life, as her patients were her
number one priority. She lived on the grounds, about two
kilometres away from the Centre. She'd never married or
had any children. All she needed was her work. Her friends
often complained to her about her workaholic tendencies
but she paid them no mind. She was unapologetic. She
was married to her practice. She didn't care much for how
taken aback people were at her reluctance to get married
and her refusal to start a family. Despite the idea that
society tries to jam down people's throats that all little
girls play with dolls and fantasize about being wives, then
grow up to have their dream weddings, become mothers
and spend their lives serving the will of their husbands,
she never once had the desire for any of that. Her work

was her life. The Centre was her baby and psychology was her husband.

ǀNamgu threw herself on the all too familiar couch and stared up at the ceiling while Dr Paul took a seat in her usual chair, and the receptionist brought them a fresh pot of green tea.

'Talk to me... What happened today?' Dr Paul had thought that because they had had such a deep session the last time, she would give her patient some time before they saw each other again, but life had other plans, as it usually does.

'Sophia came to see me. Hotani brought her here. I blame her. You know, if it wasn't for her, I wouldn't even have been at the party.'

'I still don't get what you mean. Last time you mentioned that she made you go, how exactly did she do that?' Blaming everyone except the rapist was very common amongst rape victims and it was time that ǀNamgu was made aware of the truth. The rapist was wrong. He was the monster; he was to blame, ultimately, wholly and completely.

'What do you mean? I told you, she begged me to go to the party, and she told me that I needed to loosen up, that I deserved a wild night out – so I humoured her.'

'And what did you make of it at the time? Because what I'm hearing is that she thought you deserved some down time. It sounds to me like she was looking out for you in a way. What do you think?' *You can plant a seed, but whether it sprouts and blooms or not, isn't up to you,* she thought to herself.

'Yeah, okay, fine, yes, she wanted me to have a good time. Her intentions were good, maybe, I don't know. Maybe she just wanted to have a good time and didn't want to go out alone.'INamgu was starting to grow irritated with the therapist, *Why is she taking Sofia's side? I'm the patient here, not her.*

'I see, but you had also said to me before how outgoing Sophia is – that she regularly went out without you, so maybe her intentions were good after all.' Dr Paul picked up her cup of tea and drank indulgently, placed the cup back onto the table before her and looked back up at INamgu.

'Ok, so maybe her intentions were good but her execution was messy. She knows I'm not a big drinker, she should've taken better care of me. She should've taken me home, made sure that I was alright. She's my best friend and she just forgot about me! She was supposed to protect me. She should've been there for me, with me. If she had been, then it never would have happened. I wouldn't have been raped.' INamgu's irritation turned to sadness and the tears welled in her eyes threatening to come spilling down her face at any moment.

'INamgu, she might have been drunk too, ever consider that? And at the end of the day the only *shouldn't* is that that man shouldn't have followed you, talked to you, touched you or forced himself onto you. But he did. *He* did that to you, not Sophia, not you, not the alcohol, not the clothes you were wearing, or your presence at a party – but him. He is the only one to blame here, and to shift blame not only causes the end of a beautiful friendship, and a pillar of strength to you, but also lets him off the hook; does that sit well with you? Is that something that you're okay with?'

INamgu uncrossed her arms and blinked away the tears that brimmed in her eyes. 'No, no! I don't want to let him off the hook and I don't want what he did to take Sophia or anything else away from me. I can't forgive her though, I can't, she abandoned me. What type of friend is she? She was supposed to be looking out for me! Why are you taking her side anyway? You don't even know her. I'm your client, not her and yet here you sit making excuses for her, trying to distract me from my anger toward her. Why are you doing that?' The tears were back. They couldn't be stopped, not by blinking, not by the swift movement of wiping her wrist over her eyes, nothing could stop the tears, not in that moment and those to follow.

'I'm not making excuses for her. You know I'm not. You're projecting, |Namgu, you're the one trying to avoid, push aside, run away – why hadn't you brought her up in this way during our previous sessions? You are right about one thing, though – I am here for you. You are my client and right now what I see is that my client is carrying a ton of anger in her heart, anger that is eating away at her soul, anger that has a stench about it, anger that, like all types of anger, poisons its carrier and not the one to whom it is directed, as the carrier would so wish it to be, no. The anger is the one thing that you are still clinging onto and you know why. Tell me! Let's hear it, and say it out loud.' More challenging was required, Dr Paul knew that. *She's strong, she can take it, she has the mind of a therapist herself – insightful, analytical, open. She knows the way; she just needs a bit of a push.*

Dr Paul's mind was working with haste, and desperation and excitement. She knew that after this |Namgu would be free, but first she would have to let the anger go. Hold on to the friendship, and let go of the anger. She drank from her tea and waited for |Namgu to speak.

128

'I worked through everything else, except the anger, that's the only thing keeping me here. Once the anger is gone I'll have to leave, face the world again, see people, answer their questions about my whereabouts, and what will I tell them? Do I have to recount the story of my rape over and over and over again? Must I relive it every time I bump into someone that heard of my pathetic attempt at suicide? For how long will I be the talk of the town? Am I the talk of the town? Does anybody even care? And what about him? Will I ever see him again?' Namgu kicked her feet up and curled up on the couch in a foetal position, the tears trickling onto the pillow resting beneath her.

'It's scary, isn't it? But what makes you think or feel like you owe anyone an explanation? Most of the people that seem to matter to you already know everything, including Sophia now, and if you like, I could write to your university lecturers. I won't give away any details but it should be enough to have them allow you to sit for special examinations if you like. Other than that, you don't owe anyone else an explanation. You can keep it all to yourself, or make up a story about where you've been, or share your story; as long as you make the choice that suits you best, the one that you feel will do you the most good. Your life, your story. You're the director and the producer, you get to decide who plays a role, how big or small their role is, what story line you follow, who the stars are, who the extras are and how you deal with the villains too. But before we get to the main scoundrel, let's talk about Tangeni for a bit? You mentioned some concern about seeing him again. Am I right to assume that you were referring to him?'

Dr Paul was all the things that make up a good therapist, things that go beyond higher education and titles, things that existed at her very core; she was always gentle when the need arose but knew exactly when to challenge to bring about transformative healing in her patients.

'I like the idea of making something up. I could say I was in back in Joburg, visiting old friends? Yeah, that's what I'll say. In the end it doesn't matter what I tell them anyway. In this city most people only pretend to show concern when all they're really looking for is a juicy story, a little bit of drama to spice up their mediocre existence. They want to be the source of all the latest gossip, the owner of the pot that pours out the most sought after tea. I couldn't care less about the opinions of the likes of those types of people. It's disgusting and Windhoek has them crawling around every corner like the city rats in New York; but it sickens me that a part of me actually does care.' INamgu sighed heavily, drank from her cup of tea until it was empty and continued. 'Yeah, you're right, as always.' She rolled her eyes and they both laughed a little. 'I was referring to Tangeni. That night, when he came to get me, I expected something from him, something that I knew he wasn't capable of... I expected empathy. He's never had the capacity to feel empathy toward anything or anyone that fell outside the bounds of his religion, his church, his God. He always tried to pressure me into giving my life to Christ and I could never tell him that I wasn't even sure if I believed in all that stuff. I think maybe that's why he was actually with me: I was already half way there – a virgin, pure, innocent, and worthy of him. All I needed was to be saved. He was always fishing for Jesus, and for him, I was the biggest fish.' She laughed.

'And what was he to you, why were you with him?'

'I don't know, in the end we were together for so long, I got comfortable. I was used to him, I knew him. I didn't love him, although I thought I did. I don't know… I guess I liked the idea of someone wanting to save me. It's weird, and I don't know how to explain. I just thought that somehow it made me a better person, being with someone who was better than me. Being close to someone who believed in something with the conviction of a Catholic priest, that shit made me feel good, like if someone like that could love me and believe in me. Perhaps my ability to live up to this holy ideal of myself made me better than I actually was.'

'Was? Do you think you're better now?'

'Yes! I am. I'm stronger. I played that recording over and over every night before bed since you gave it to me. At first it hurt, it really hurt; it was excruciating. It felt as though my soul was being ripped into a billion pieces. It hurt so bad to hear myself, my voice cracking, the tears muffling my words, the pain swallowing me whole, the memories, the visuals, seeing him – hearing his disgusting grunts in my ears – the tears. The tears that poured out of me, emptying every inch of me, making me feel like all the joy inside me was being spilled over and over again – it was hell. I went through hell. The fire and flames ate at me, burning everything in sight. I was submerged, I was in hell and the devil himself reached up from beneath the earth and dragged me deeper into hell and all I wanted to do was to fucking die. But then my mom came and found me – we had plans to spend the day together a couple of weeks back. She must've been so shocked when she let herself in and saw me that way. Anyways, I woke up and I heard my sister tell a nurse off for me. For the first time she stood up for me and when they thought I was asleep, I heard my mother telling me that she loved me and that she was proud of me. Even my dad showed up for me and then I met you. I was so angry, so hurt, so sad, and you just sat in that chair drinking your green tea and there it was, there I was. Your image reflected and embodied a vision of me: whole and healed. And that's when I knew that I couldn't die. I didn't want to die anymore and I found meaning and purpose in this shit storm that forced its way onto my skin and into my body and I felt hope again because I knew what I had to do, what I have to do.'

ǀNamgu was sitting up now and her words emerged through a smile that had been forming on her face.

Dr Paul felt a warmth in her heart. She knew the answer, but she had to ask, the way therapists always seem to do.

'And what is that? What is it that gave you hope, meaning and purpose?' She smiled at ǀNamgu with her eyes wide.

'I have to drop out of the arts and pursue psychology with all that is left within me. I need to nurture what's already within me and use it to help others like me – the ones whose wounds have torn holes into their souls.'

'That's very beautiful, ǀNamgu. Just be sure to give yourself time to focus on yourself for a while. Don't rush into anything. You're allowed to take things slowly. Just take things one day at a time. For starters, I offer a series of trauma management sessions online that I'd like you to join. I teach meditation, deep breathing and other relaxation techniques that I think you're ready to start learning and implementing in your daily life. These tools, as well as everything else we've shared in our sessions will always be there for you, whenever you need them.'

And with that, the session had come to an end. Dr Paul explained to |Namgu that they would no longer need to see each other as often and that she was welcome to stay at the Centre for a few more weeks until she felt ready to leave. She emphasized that |Namgu could always call her, or come and see her at the Centre if she ever felt stuck.

~

Two weeks had passed since her last session. It was late in the day and |Namgu took a slow stroll in the garden taking care to look intently at each plant and breathe deeply in the warm air that surrounded her. She had asked Dr Paul to call Sophia and ask her to come back to the Centre a couple of times. They reconnected and caught up interminably.

They met in the garden, quite a distance away from the big glass doors leading into the visitor's area, because it was getting really hot during this time of the year and not many people opted to sit out in the garden after lunch time. They preferred the air-conditioned indoors. |Namgu pulled the tape recorder from her jacket pocket and handed it to Sophia who pressed play and cried with the same type of intensity with which |Namgu had found herself crying since she woke up at the Centre, the tears which seemed as though they would never stop falling from her face. When she was done listening, she hugged |Namgu and held onto her for dear life, for what seemed like forever.

'I'm so sorry, for everything. I would take your place in a heartbeat if I could. Please know that.' Sophia finally understood everything: the suicide attempt, the reluctance of the Swaartboois to have Sophia see her, ǀNamgu's outburst two weeks ago, everything finally made sense.

'No, don't you dare pick up the anger that I harboured against you. This wasn't your fault – the only one to blame is him and we can't let him tear us apart. He has no power over us, not anymore.' She hugged her friend once more and prayed that the anger would fall away from her heart as easily as the tears had been falling from her face.

~

As the days went by, ǀNamgu felt stronger, both emotionally and physically; she was ready to leave the Centre. On the day that she was leaving, as her sister's red Polo pulled away from the Centre, ǀNamgu saw Angel in the rear-view mirror yelling,

'They taking things from you, they take things they shouldn't but we taking back what's ours, we taking back what's ours, we taking back what's ours.'

Eighteen

It had been the first time after months that she'd been left alone by everyone – her parents, her sister, and Sophia and Khoendi – who had now become inseparable. Even Dr Paul's weekly phone calls had ceased and ǀNamgu felt relieved. It had been almost a year now. She had regularly attended a support group for rape victims and she had had the opportunity to write her exams and obtained a first class pass in the psychology program. Since leaving the wellness centre she had regularly written to Dr Paul telling her of her travels.

Perhaps it was out of guilt or perhaps her parents had some supressed desire to escape the busyness of their lives, but for their own reasons, they had funded and accommodated her every whim, which included trips to Damaraland to visit the homeland of the author who had written the series of books she had so loved as a teenager, and Walvis Bay where she climbed one of the highest desert dunes in the world and sat at its peak, filling her lungs with gulps of salty coastal air, swimming in the ocean afterwards.

Her trips also included a stop in the Eastern Cape where she'd gone to school before having moved back to Namibia

– where she learned that she had outgrown the place but spent hours every day breathing in the potential of the city of Makhanda. She travelled to Cape Town where she enjoyed stuffing her face with foods from all over the world along Long Street or lying on Camps Bay beach, soaking up the sun when the confusing weather allowed for it. From there she ventured off to Zimbabwe where she went deep sea diving to see if the myths surrounding the Chinhoyi caves were really true; a part of her wanted the myths to be true – that mer-people would drag her into the depths of the underground ocean where she would ultimately drown and be swallowed up. She also allowed the Victoria Falls to completely soak her clothing, after refusing to wear a rain coat on the hike. She wanted to feel everything. Her parents were relieved that she was up and about, living, adventuring, taking back her life, and they were happy to accompany her on her travels; in fact, they gave her no choice.

Dr Paul had advised that she should not be left to her own devices for extended periods of time for about two months after being discharged from the centre. Failed suicide attempts were often followed by another, so precautions had to be taken, even though Dr Paul was confident that ǀNamgu would be just fine; it was standard procedure to caution the family. Finally, ǀNamgu was off suicide watch and her family stopped taking turns to spend time at her place or have her over at theirs when she wasn't traveling. Sophia had moved in with Khoendi, and ǀNamgu moved into a smaller place nearer to her parents' home.

It was Easter weekend and most Windhoekers had left the city for the long weekend as the air in the city grew stale and so people ventured out to breathe in the cold air of the

Atlantic Ocean along the coast, or up north to drink in the beautiful smell of the *oshanas* and help out at their villages, or returned to the south to visit old wrinkly, grandparents. A beautiful silence covered the city and INamgu loved it. She walked up the street to the Bougainville's on Sam Nujoma Drive and had a hearty sirloin steak washed down with half a bottle of merlot. She had dessert and took the rest of the bottle to go. She walked home feeling satisfied and peaceful. The warmth of the day had passed and some birds were flying overhead. One or two cars drove past her and the chatter of nannies on their way home from work could be heard from across the street. She loved the smell of the light summer rain on the ground and she breathed it in hungrily.

When she got home she placed her handbag on the coffee table, opened the bottle of wine and drank straight from the bottle. She pulled out the journal that she used to send letters to Dr Paul and wrote:

Death is but a door leading to sweet serenity, complete equilibrium of mind, body and soul that the body yearns for after years of pain and suffering that plague life so relentlessly. The nightmares linger, the tears flow heedlessly. Even as I sleep, I still see him in everything and everyone. His face is etched into the insides of my eyelids, even as I travelled to escape his smell in the city air. He haunts my entire existence and invades my every thought. I sometimes wonder if perhaps some wounds cannot be healed. The thought of this being a very real possibility scares me but something else inside me wants to keep fighting for myself, to keep going, to not let men like him win, to not let what happened to me define

me or be the end but to keep fighting, not only for myself but
also for thousands of brilliantly strong women just like me,
and that flicker of hope somehow keeps me going.

By the time she had finished writing her letter, the wine bottle was empty. The sea of sadness within her had become like an old companion. It ebbed and flowed inside her regardless of how desperately she clung to any hope, or promise, or glimpse of happiness.

She thought back to her group therapy sessions, of all the women that she'd encountered there in the Old Catholic church in Pioneers' Park where they'd meet every Wednesday. The support group had been recommended to her by Dr Paul upon termination of therapy with her. She had told |Namgu that many rape victims benefit immensely from joining support groups or from the experience of group therapy. |Namgu disagreed. For her, hearing all the awful stories shared by her fellow group members seemed to make her feel even worse about what had happened to her and to them. At times, sessions left her feeling guilty for being in such bad shape after rape because some of the stories she'd heard had been about women who had been raped continuously by their father or uncle for years until they ran away from home to fend for themselves; stories about how their own mothers would kick them out of their homes for bringing such allegations against their beloved husbands; stories of violent rapes – where the rapist would beat their victim half to death whilst forcing himself inside her. It was all too awful and what was worst for her was the fact that the facilitator of the sessions, Ms Shimutwikeni, had been a rape victim herself.

Nineteen

INamgu's thoughts and memories moved her to tears. She sat and cried until her body buckled and she fell to the floor. She cried until her eyes burned, her nose clogged up and her chest hurt as she gasped for air. Her body shook violently as she wrapped her arms tightly around her belly as though to comfort herself or rather, in a bid to hold herself together because it felt as though she was falling apart, losing herself, coming undone. She feared her physical being would fall apart the way that her inner world had been shattered. It felt as though she had been lying on the floor for hours until a single salty tear trickled down her face, burned her cheek and landed on her lips. She licked her lips and the taste was reminiscent of that of the Atlantic Ocean. Her eyes shut as the childhood memory came flooding in...

It was one of the days in Swakopmund where the skies cleared up and the fog disappeared. The sky was vast and blue and spotless; not a single cloud could be seen. The gulls soared across the clear blue sky as the sun fiercely warmed the golden sand. The sound of children's laughter, splashes and chatter lingered in the air and a vibrantly blissful energy buzzed between the sky and the sea.

/Namgu's parents sat on the bright red circular beach towel that doubled as a picnic blanket, large enough to host the family of four and a few picnic baskets on it too. It was spread out over the glistening beach sand that twinkled beneath them. They talked and giggled over cold slices of refreshing watermelon, glancing up and waving at /Namgu and Hotani every now and then. They weren't too worried about the safety of their children in the sea as both of their daughters swam at competitive levels and were used to braving the ocean waters. The presence of the lifeguard in red swim shorts perched on his chair towering over the ocean also comforted them and allowed them to relax.

/Namgu had always loved the ocean deeply. Its calm yet potentially deadly or violent nature fascinated her. Hotani loved to swim, but hated the idea of seaweed brushing her feet, so she sat on the beach sand building sand castles, close enough to watch the waves swaying back and forth, yet far enough not to get her feet wet. /Namgu was knee-deep in the water, being rocked to and fro.

'We should stop letting her roam and swim in the ocean so freely. It's dangerous, we'll live to regret it someday.' Mr Swaartbooi groaned to his wife after spitting some watermelon seeds into the palm of his hand, with a stern look on his face, not knowing just how wrong and simultaneously how right he was.

'She's an excellent swimmer, relax. Besides, we've been letting her do this since forever. Just let her be.' She was in awe of her daughter's fearlessness and the strength with which she took on the wild Atlantic Ocean, amongst other things. It was a gorgeous day. The sky was clear, the sun was shining, not a breeze of moving air brushed their skin and Hatago Swaartbooi didn't want to ruin it with unnecessary worry.

/Namgu's feet were sinking into the drenched ocean sand beneath the water like quick sand and the waves pulled her in deeper and

140

deeper until she allowed her feet to rise. As they rose, she kicked them violently, swimming toward the raft 150 m ahead of her. The water hugged and engulfed her and it felt as though she were part of the ocean. The ocean was strong, powerful, yet calmly pushing her toward the safety of the raft. She knew the ocean was not to be toyed with, nor was it to be underestimated, for its power could engulf any woman or man in a matter of seconds.

While she floated, ǁNamgu felt that all too familiar sensation of dizziness and disorientation that her childhood orthostatic hypotension sometimes brought about, but that she had never experienced in a moment where it could literally end her life.

'Not right now, please not now', she thought.

But her blood pressure did not seem to hear nor care that she preferred not to have another fainting spell even if she would surely drown in the ocean if she did. She felt light headed, almost floating in and out of consciousness and her vision became distorted. Her body felt too heavy for her arms and legs to keep above water and she felt herself sinking slightly.

'NO, not like this!' She made the mental declaration. She told herself very sternly and directed all her mental effort toward willing her legs to kick and her arms to paddle.

'You can do this, you can do this, you can do this, you can do this...' She allowed the words to repeat over and over again until she started to believe them, and felt them deep within her heart and soul. The next thing she knew, a friendly stranger's hairy arm waited to pull her up to safety on the raft. She lay on her back, soaking up the warmth of the sun, the wooden raft floating gently, rocking up and down and side to side, all at the same time.

'You can do this, you can do this, you can do this, you can do this.' The words stirred something in her spirit: hope, will, persistence, strength and courage. They started off as mental chatter from a not so distant memory and then she began chanting them, softly at first and then like explosions that seem to stitch the broken parts of her back together until her tears dried. It was as though she had been face to face with a brick wall that stopped her from seeing or feeling anything other than her pain, her trauma, her wounds. The memory of her strength turned her around, to awaken to what lay beyond that wall. A wave of energy hit her, as if her will to live had been struck back into her mind, body and soul like a lightning bolt, surging through her. She felt alive again, for the first time in a very, very long time. If she hadn't allowed the power and force of the majestic ocean to overpower her, she would not allow a man to snatch her life, her happiness, herself from herself either.

She remembered the strength, warmth and willingness to share emulated by the women in the support group. She remembered the renewed loving care and the tenderness that her family had shown her. She pondered the depth of the friendship that she shared with Sophia.

She thought of the hope and healing that the future presented but mostly, she remembered herself. She remembered the girl who had a pristine affinity for books, the one who cherished friendship and moved as though she breathed performance art and dreamed of growing into an empathic drama therapist. Her conception of herself came pouring in like rain, after years of drought, plentiful and nourishing, filling her up and transcending into a feeling of hope and healing that brought her will to live back to life. She realised that there was one fatal flaw in her escape theory – she didn't actually want to die, she was just afraid of living. She had held onto her fear and anxiety for so long that it had almost swallowed her whole. Dread had become her comfort zone and the thought of being torn away from it was exactly what had been driving her suicidal thoughts and intention.

Rape is a vile and violent act with the potential to wrench the soul right out of a person. Like being murdered over and over again, the act in itself takes the life from its victim. Rape robs its victim of their sense of control and even of the very thing gods of all religions dare not interfere with — free will and freedom of choice. Even though all this was true, INamgu realised that nothing outside of herself could truly conquer her soul, not without her permission and certainly not without a fight. And she was right, we cannot control extrinsic forces, like hurricanes and tornados, which come without warning and may tear down all that we have grown and built, but they cannot touch our will to live or the purpose and meaning that we find within our lives.

INamgu sat up and saw the copy of the book she'd got from Tanaka lying on her coffee table. She took the book in her hands and leafed through it with searching eyes. First she stopped on the page where Tanaka had left his phone number and saved it on her phone; she would call him later.

Then she opened the book on page one hundred and sixteen and read the words in the paragraph titled 'Post-Traumatic Transcendence':

To experience trauma and suffering is inevitable. It is an event or situation that has not yet been resolved within ourselves to a point of triumph or transcendence. Not all traumas are equal — some require more attention and healing, like experiencing an assault or natural disaster, and others are seemingly everyday life events like sibling rivalry or a stressful work situation. All types of trauma, however, demand and deserve attention especially from within because you are wholly your own. Each wound contains an intrinsic wisdom that allows for a deeper knowing of yourself, a lesson about self-healing and an opportunity to love and transcend yourself beyond your pain.

Of all her existential ponderings, what stood out most was the realisation that it wasn't that she didn't want to die, but rather that the ratio of her will to live now far outweighed her desire to die, and she had a feeling that her life was worth a thousand second chances.

Additional Resources

The following section offers insight about various mental health issues such as suicide, rape and depression as well as tips regarding how one can recognise, prevent or take action when faced with these very real life challenges or trauma.

Suicide

Whether you've read about it in the papers, or have lost someone close to you, or even struggled with suicide ideation yourself, one thing is for sure: suicide is serious and should not be swept under the rug. In an article in the *Windhoek Observer*, Shaun Whittaker, a Namibian clinical psychologist, stated that there is a suicide crisis in the country (Nhongo, 2017). We need to enlighten ourselves and those around us about what suicide is, how it's preventable and openly discuss warning signs as well as inform each other about the help that is available for those suffering from thoughts of and intentions to commit suicide. The more openly and honestly we share, the more closely we can connect to and understand each other and ultimately, prevent deaths by suicide, because awareness is always the first step towards healing.

Warning signs of suicide

Here are a few warning signs of suicide to look out for in yourself through self-awareness, as well as in your loved ones, by making an effort and checking in on them regularly:

1. Appearing depressed and sad or regularly displaying a low mood. (Untreated clinical depression can often lead to suicide)
2. Feeling and expressing hopelessness
3. Social and emotional withdrawal from friends and family
4. Sleeping too much or too little
5. Preparing for death (giving away possessions, writing a will)
6. Engaging in suicidal talk (statements such as, "I want to die", "Everyone would be better off without me")
7. Gaining or losing significant amounts of weight
8. Losing interest in hobbies or previously enjoyed activities
9. Feelings of excessive guilt or shame
10. Behaving extremely recklessly
11. Poor performance in work and school
12. Drug and alcohol abuse

These are just a few examples of warning signs to look out for. Many people, however, tend to hide their depression or thoughts of suicide because there is still a strong social stigma around mental illness, so it may be hard to detect, but not impossible. Suicide can have many causes, and is often challenging to pin down to just one single cause. Here are a couple of possible causes:

1. Untreated depression or other mental illness
2. Negative or stressful life events (death of a loved one, divorce, terminal illness, being victimised, feeling trapped or hopeless, bullying)

Take extra care to look out for warning signs and possible causal factors, and always take suicidal talk or ideation very seriously. Encourage yourself or your loved one/s to get the help that they deserve, without judging them or getting angry with them.

There are various mental health services available in Namibia that can offer counselling and support when dealing with issues that could lead to suicide or suicidal intentions. Please reach out to receive the professional attention that you and your loved ones deserve.

Rape

Gender Based Violence (GBV) can be defined as an act or acts that almost always result in physical, sexual or psychological harm or suffering. GBV includes physical rape or other sexually abusive acts, intimate partner violence and genital mutilation.

Most death and disability in women and girls aged between 15 to 44 years is a result of violence against women. Gender Based Violence (GBV) is more life threatening than cancer, road accidents and malaria. Namibia has one of the highest rates of GBV in the entire Southern African Development Community region (Friedrich Ebert Stiftung, 2015). Although most of the focus is on female victims, males can and do also fall prey to GBV. The efforts of Government, the Namibian police force, health care providers, schools or Gender Based Violence Investigation Units should all be in line with the Vision 2030 strategy of Namibia. The common goal should be directed toward prevention of GBV and support as well as protection of survivors.

Rape can be defined as the violent act by which sexual penetration is forced onto a person. The grotesque and exceedingly violent act involves inflicting pain, humiliation and suffering, and is largely seen as an enforcement of power. Rape is one of the most vile and devastating assaults that can be inflicted upon a person. Oftentimes, rapes are an indication of severe aggressive, antisocial acts carried out by one who lacks empathy. Rape can be unplanned assaults that take place in conjunction with other criminal activity such as robbery. However, rapes can also be well thought out and planned assaults resulting from anger and vindictiveness against specific women or vulnerable groups. There are different types of rape, namely corrective rape, date rape, marital rape and child rape.

The victim of rape should never be shamed or blamed for the act of rape, for the only thing that causes rape is a rapist and what perpetuates it in the minds of its perpetrators is a rape culture within society that endorses rape and other sexual acts, especially against women and other vulnerable and unsuspecting groups within society. Often, education and information about rape revolves around how victims can prevent rape or stay safe. Advice ranges from encouraging women to dress more modestly, to avoid certain areas at certain times of night, and so forth. This type of advice can be misleading and harmful in that it perpetuates the idea that victims somehow are to be blamed and shamed for dressing provocatively or for acting in a sexually suggestive manner, which is the furthest thing from the truth. Education about rape should involve alterations in gender norms, and information about consent and its importance. The culture of silence surrounding sex and sexuality in Namibia is also a detrimental factor, as our cultures generally don't allow for people to talk openly about these pertinent issues.

Each victim and survivor of rape is entitled to and will experience their own reaction to sexual violence. Some might be more open to share and express their feelings about the rape, others might be reluctant to talk about or even report the incident. The devastating consequences of rape make for a long index of health concerns, including unwanted pregnancies, HIV/AIDS, sexually transmitted infections, physical consequences such as altered eating or sleeping patterns, substance abuse and physical injury, mental problems such as nightmares, flashbacks, depression and Post-Traumatic Stress Disorder, and emotional suffering (guilt, shame and self-blame). Because of all its adverse effects, recovery can be exceedingly challenging but it is a possible although slow process.

Actions to Take If You've Been Raped

1. Try to avoid washing your body or getting rid of clothing worn during the time of your rape, as this may destroy or damage evidence that could be used in your case against the rapist, should you lay a charge with the police.

2. See your nearest doctor, clinic or hospital to receive proper medical attention, which could include:
   - Post-exposure prophylaxis (PEP), if taken within 48 hours of the rape, is a medication available to rape victims that can prevent HIV infection.
   - Pills to prevent unwanted pregnancy can be prescribed; options to maintain the pregnancy are also available.
   - Physical injuries and wounds incurred during the rape can be treated.

- Counselling services may be made available for emotional and psychological recovery.
3. In Namibia, you can open a case or lay a charge with the police in the Women and Child Protection Unit. This can help to bring the rapist to justice and also prevent him or her from raping someone else. Reporting your rapist isn't always the easiest thing to do, so try to have a supportive friend or family accompany you. Also, if you don't feel ready or willing to lay a charge against the rapist, people around you should respect that decision too.

Depression

Mood disorders, as the name implies, affect our moods and emotions. Depression is a disorder that influences thoughts, actions and behaviours of those suffering from it. Depression occurs on a scale and ranges from mild to severe, depending on its intensity. The Diagnostic and Statistical Manual of Mental Disorders (America Psychiatric Association, 2013) describes several types of depressive disorders. These differ in frequency and symptoms as well as severity. According to Barlow and Durand (2012), the most frequently diagnosed as well as most severe form of depression is referred to as a major depressive disorder. This form of depression is marked by persistent feelings of sadness and a lack of motivation. Symptoms include increased sleep, weight loss/gain, morbid or suicidal thoughts, and withdrawal from loved ones as well as from activities previously regarded as desirable.

If you suspect that you or a loved one is suffering from depression, seek the help or gently urge your loved one to seek the help of a Mental Health Professional in order to receive a clinical diagnosis as well as the appropriate treatment. More details of the signs or symptoms of a major depressive disorder are listed below. Please note that at least five symptoms must be present and last for a period of about two weeks or more.

Criteria or Symptoms of Depression:
1. Low or depressed mood for most of the day, or nearly half the day, indicated by feelings of sadness and emptiness.
2. Feelings of hopelessness, worthlessness and excessive guilt.
3. Wanting to die or commit suicide.
4. Lack of or low levels of energy; a continuous state of fatigue.
5. Changes in sleeping patterns (insomnia – sleeping too little, hypersomnia – sleeping too much).
6. Change in diet or eating habits; eating too much or too little, and gaining or losing weight as a result.
7. Significant weight loss or gain when not dieting, as well as significant changes in appetite, almost on a daily basis.
8. Lack of or low level of motivation.
9. No or little desire to engage in hobbies or previously enjoyed activities. Taking no or little interest or pleasure in most activities, most of the day, nearly every day.
10. Crying often or appearing tearful.

The Mental Health Professional will use a special book called the Diagnostic and Statistics Manual of Mental Disorders (American Psychiatric Association, Fifth Edition, 2013) as well as counselling interviews or sessions and perhaps psychometrics in order to make a diagnosis. When making a diagnosis, medical professionals and mental health professionals work together to rule out other conditions that may cause you to display similar symptoms, such as thyroid problems or vitamin deficiencies.

Risk Factors for Depression can include genetics, environmental factors or personality factors and treatment can involve psychotherapy, medication and various psychosocial approaches.

Mental Health

When we talk about health and wellness, the things that most commonly come to mind are the aspects of health pertaining to fitness, hydrating and exercise. What we tend to overlook is mental or psychological health, which is quite a contradiction because the very definition of health stresses the various aspects, including mental health. This definition reinforces the statement that there is no health without mental health.

When we neglect mental health, we are ignoring our inner voice, our emotions, the impact that our interactions have on one another, the possibility of reaching our fullest potential and most importantly, the fact that each of us deserves help and healing when our mental health is compromised. Sweeping mental illness under the proverbial rug only leads to the continuation and acceleration of stereotypes and thus, the isolation of those living with mental health issues. As bad as it may be to live with mental health issues which can range from mood disorders to personality disorders, it doesn't have to be all doom and gloom (even though it may feel that way at times). Also, you don't have to have a mental illness in order to take care of your mental health and wellness. Getting clued up on the various ways that enhance mental health, especially those more easily accessible to most people, can also help you to extend loving care to those around you who may need it. Taking care of your mental health and that of those around you can help you become mentally strong, more calm and confident and boost your overall sense of wellbeing. Here are some ways to nurture mental health:

1. Check in on yourself and your loved ones
A little introspection can go a very long way. Self-analysis is not only free but also offers a wealth of benefits. When you check in on yourself regularly to assess your level of emotional and psychological wellbeing, it's easier to identify areas that are neglected and then make the necessary adjustments to work on those areas. Checking in on your loved ones is a selfless act that in turns boosts your wellbeing and lets them know that there's someone in this world who cares that they are alive and well.

2. Spend time in nature
Our environment has an impact on our wellbeing. There's a whole branch of therapy called Eco therapy that emphasises and uses nature as a therapeutic tool. The University of Essex undertook a study and published a report in 2007 that found that almost 70 per cent of people undergo notifiable increases in wellbeing following eco therapy (https://www.mind.org.uk). Eco therapy involves spending time in nature, possibly taking up various activities such as hiking, mountain bike riding or gardening (Mind, 2018). I reckon it would do us a lot of good to "stop and smell the flowers" at every

chance we get. Just to gaze upon a clear blue sky, or to kick off your shoes and feel the sand or grass between your toes or feel the wind against your skin will help you unwind from your day. Nature has always played a vital role in the lives of people, from inspiring creativity to supporting basic survival. Nature can also be extremely therapeutic, proven by emerging psychotherapy practices like Eco therapy. The best thing about it is that it is absolutely free.

3. Practice the attitude of gratitude

Giving thanks and expressing gratitude for all the things that we are fortunate to have in our lives should become a daily habit. Compton and Hoffman (2013) assert that research indicates that the expression of gratitude contributes to wellbeing by showing us the social support we have. It also lowers stress and mitigates depression. Gratitude should become engraved in our daily thought process because it feels good to think about the positive things that we have in our lives, or about the people whom we love. Also, the more we value and appreciate the things that mean the most to us, the more we take care of them, which adds even more value to them which, in turn, enhances our sense of gratitude for them. The key to reaping the benefits of gratitude is not only to feel gratitude but to actively express it. So when someone does something nice for you, thank them, no matter how small the gesture. It's not only polite, it also boosts your sense of wellbeing.

4. Get active

Incorporating a regular work-out into your daily routine is not only beneficial for your physical body, but also for your mental and emotional health (Morgen & Goldston, 2013). Exercise boosts neural growth, releases feel-good chemicals in your body known as endorphins and can serve as a mindfulness practice and as such, breaks cycles of negative thoughts. Regular exercise can also regulate sleep patterns, and practising yoga, gentle stretching or meditation in bed can help you relax and improve your quality of sleep. Pederson and Saltin (2015) provide a considerable amount of evidence which encourages regular physical activity such as running, hiking and swimming as exercise to serve as a natural, inexpensive and easily accessible means for coping with mental stress, depression and anxiety.

5. Rest and relax

Make sure that you're getting enough hours of sleep (6 to 8 hours a night) to avoid fatigue and moods swings as a result of too little sleep. Also try to seek out and engage in activities that enhance your sense of inner stillness and peace through relaxation. According to Weiten (2007), relaxation techniques such as meditation or the relaxation procedure described by Benson et al. (1975) are associated with beneficial effects on self-esteem, mood, sense of control and overall well-being. Ancient yogis discovered the power of breath or pranayama (energy control) aeons ago and many people are still using deep breathing techniques to help them relax, enter meditative states and relieve stress. Deep breathing can help shift the focus of an anxious, overthinking mind and bring a sense of inner stillness and peace to a tense body.

These small and simple ways are not meant to replace psychotherapy or psychopharmaceutic treatments offered by mental health professionals, but rather, to be used in conjunction with conventional treatment. These methods can be used in everyday life situations by everyday people at no cost, meaning they are easily accessible to us all and can go a long way towards maintaining and even enhancing mental health. If you're struggling, and suspect that you might have troubles with regards to your mental health, then it is imperative that you refrain from self-diagnosing and rather make an appointment with your general practitioner. A medical doctor or psychiatrist can advise you on the most suitable mode of treatment for you which might include counselling with a psychologist or psychological counsellor.

The Psychological Association of Namibia has an online database of psychological counsellors and psychologists all over Namibia. If you or a loved one are in need of professional help, the database is available on their website at http://www.psychologynamibia.org/find-a-practitioner-near-you/

References

American Psychiatric Association. (2013). *Diagnostic and Statistical Manual of Mental Disorders* (5th ed.). Arlington, VA: American Psychiatric Association.

Barlow, D. & Durand, V. (2012). *Abnormal Psychology: an Integrative Approach.* California: Wadsworth Publishing Company.

Benson, H., Greenwood, M. M., & Klemchuk, H. (1975). The Relaxation Response: Psychophysiologic Aspects and Clinical Applications. *The International Journal of Psychiatry in Medicine, 6*(1–2), 87–98. https://doi.org/10.2190/376W-E4MT-QM6Q-H0UM

Mind. (2018). Nature and Mental Health. Retrieved fromhttps://www.mind.org.uk/information-support/tips-for-everyday-living//nature-and-mental-health/#.XHqdp_ZuLcc

Friedrich Ebert Stiftung. (2015). *The Voice of the Survivors.* Windhoek: Friedrich Ebert Stiftung.

Government of the Republic of Namibia. (2004). Vision 2030 Policy Framework for Longterm National Development. Windhoek: Namprint. Also available at https://gov. na.vision-2030

Nhongo, A. (2017, January 27). Namibia near top of suicide rankings. Retrieved from https://www.observer.com.na

Morgan, W. & Goldston, S. (2013). *Exercise and Mental Health*. New York: Hemisphere Publishing Corporation.

Pedersen, B.K. & Saltin, B. (2015). Exercise as medicine – Evidence for prescribing exercise as therapy in 26 different chronic diseases. *Scandinavian Journal of Medicine & Science in Sports. 25 Suppl 3*: 1-72. doi: 10.1111/sms.12581.

Weiten, W. (2007). *Psychology: themes and variations* (7th ed). Belmont, CA: Thomson/Wadsworth.

Printed in the United States
By Bookmasters